KIRSTY LOGAN
THE RENTAL HEART
AND OTHER STORIES

SALT

CROMER

PUBLISHED BY SALT PUBLISHING
12 Norwich Road, Cromer, Norfolk NR27 0AX United Kingdom

First published by Salt Publishing, 2014

Printed in Great Britain by Clays Ltd, St Ives plc

Typeset in Paperback 9.5/13

ISBN 978 1 907773 75 4 paperback

3 5 7 9 8 6 4 2

to Mama Logan

CONTENTS

ACKNOWLEDGEMENTS

'The Rental Heart' first published in *PANK #4*.

'Underskirts' first published in *Bridport Prize: The Winners 2010* (Redcliffe Press).

'A Skulk of Saints' first published as 'Underlying' in *Algebra #2*.

'The Last 3,600 Seconds' first published at circlet.com.

'The Broken West' first published in *Gutter #7*.

'Bibliophagy' first published at elimae.com.

'Coin-Operated Boys' first published at fantasybookreview. co.uk.

'Una and Coll are not Friends', 'All the Better to Eat You With', 'The Light Eater' and 'Matryoshka' all first broadcast on BBC Radio 4.

'Sleeping Beauty' first published as 'Beauty' at annalemma. com.

'Witch' first published in *Best Lesbian Erotica 2011* (Cleis Press).

'The Man From the Circus' first published at sigriddaughter. com.

'Feeding' first published as 'Feed' in *Sushirexia* (Freight).

'Origami' first published in *Let's Pretend* (Freight).

'Tiger Palace' first published in *Diva*.

THE RENTAL HEART

THE RENTAL HEART

The day after I met Grace – her pierced little mouth, her shitkicker boots, her hands as small as goosebumps writing numbers on my palm. The day after I met her, I went to the heart rental place.

I hadn't rented in years, and doubted they would have my preferred model. The window display was different, the hearts sleeker and shinier than I remembered. The first time I had rented it was considered high-tech to have the cogs tucked away; now they were as smooth and seamless as a stone. Some of the new hearts had extras I'd never seen, like timers and standby buttons and customised beating patterns.

That made me think about Grace, her ear pressed to my sternum, listening to the morse code of her name, and my own heart started to creep up my throat, so I swallowed it down and went into the shop.

An hour later I was chewing lunch and trying to read the instruction leaflet. They made it seem so complicated, but it wasn't really. The hearts just clipped in, and as long as you remembered to close yourself up tightly, then they could tick away for years. Decades, probably. The problems come when the hearts get old and scratched: shreds of past loves get caught in the dents, and they're tricky to rinse out. Even a wire brush won't do it.

But the man in the rental place had assured me that this one was factory-fresh, clean as a kitten's tongue. Those heart rental guys always lied, but I could tell by the heart's coppery sheen that it hadn't been broken yet.

I remembered perfectly well how to fit the heart, but I still read the leaflet to the end as a distraction. A way to not think about how Grace looked when she bit her lip, when she wrote the curls of her number. How she would look later tonight, when she. When we.

It was very important that I fit the heart before that happened.

∽

Ten years ago, first heart. Jacob was as solid and golden as a tilled field, and our love was going to last forever, which at our age meant six months. Every time Jacob touched me, I felt my heart thud wetly against my lungs. When I watched him sleep, I felt it clawing up my oesophagus. Sometimes it was hard to speak from the wet weight of it sitting at the base of my tongue. I would just smile and wait for him to start talking again.

The more I loved him, the heavier my heart felt, until I was walking around with my back bent and my knees cracking from the weight of it. When Jacob left, I felt my heart shatter like a shotgun pellet, shards lodging in my guts. I had to drink every night to wash the shards out. I had to.

A year later I met Anna. She was dreadlocked, greeneyed, full of verbs. She smelled of rain and revolution. I fell.

But the parts of me that I wanted to give to Anna were long gone. There was not enough left that was worth giving. The edges of my heart were jagged now, and I did not want to feel those rough edges climbing my throat. I did not love her enough to cough blood. I kept what was left of me close, tucked under the long soft coils of my intestines where Anna wouldn't see.

One night, still throbbing, Anna opened her chest. Her heart nestled, a perfect curl of clockwork.

This is how, she said.

I could hear its tick against the soft embrace of her lungs, and I bent close to her to smell its metallic sharpness. I wanted.

The next day she took me to the heart rental place. I spent a long time pressing my palms against the polished metal until I found one that felt warm against my skin. I made sure that the sharp edges of the cogs were tucked inwards, kept away from the just-healed rawness of my throat.

Back at Anna's, she unwrapped the plastic, fitted the heart, closed my chest, took me to bed. Later I watched her sleep and loved her with every cog of my heart.

When Anna ran off with my best friend, I took the heart back to the rental place. Nothing choked or shattered or weighed me down. It looked just as sleekshiny as when I had first taken it out of the wrapping, and the rental guy gave me my full deposit back. I deleted Anna's phone number and went out for dinner.

The next year, when I met Will, I knew what to do. The heart this time was smaller, more compact, and it clipped into place easily. Technology moves fast.

Will taught me about Boudicea, the golden section,

musical intervals, Middle English. I soaked him up like I was cotton wool.

Sometimes, pre-dawn, I would sneak into the bathroom and open myself to the mirror. The heart reflected Will back at me, secure in its mechanics. I would unclip it, watch it tick in my fist, then put it back before sliding into Will's arms.

On our first holiday, I beeped through the airport barriers. I showed my heart and was waved on. It wasn't until the plane was taxiing that I realised Will had not beeped. I spent the whole flight wire-jawed with my paperback open to page one, unable to stop thinking about the contents of Will's chest. We never mentioned it; I could not stand to think of his chest cavity all full of wet red flesh.

When I left Will, I returned the heart again. I couldn't sleep for the thought of his heart, shot into shards, sticking in his guts, scratching up his gullet.

After that I rented hearts for Michael, and Rose, and Genevieve. They taught me about Heisenberg's Uncertainty Principle and how to look after a sausage dog. They smelled of petrol and hair oil and sawdust and honeysuckle.

Soon the heart rental guy started to greet me by name. He gave me a bulk discount and I got invited to his Christmas party. Soon I found that halfway between sleeping and waking, the glint of the rental guy's gold incisor would flicker at the corners of my eyes. I wondered if he licked the hearts before renting them to me, so molecules of him would be caught down in some tiny hidden cog, merging into my insides.

The glint of the rental guy in my dreams started to make me uncomfortable, so I switched to a new rental place. There were plenty to choose from, and I preferred the ones that didn't gleam their teeth at me. They never gave me back my security deposits, but always kept their stares on the scratched glass counter when I returned the hearts. Their downturned eyes were more important than the shine of coins.

As I got older, the hearts got smaller. After Genevieve I moved away for a while, to an island where I knew no one and nothing, not even the language. I lived alone. I did not need to rent a heart. My empty chest made it easy to breathe, and I filled my lungs with the sharp air of the sea. I stayed there for a year.

Back in the city, back in the world. Among words and faces I knew. One night, many drinks, and Grace's number scrawled tiny on my skin. The sleekshiny new heart.

I swallowed the rest of my lunch and went home to fit the heart.

Three years later, Autumn afternoon, curled on the couch with newsprint on my fingers and Grace's dozing hair in my lap. A small notice in the corner of the page:

Product recall: Heart Model #345-27J. Defective.

I pressed my hand – the hand holding the dark length of Grace's hair – against my chest. I hadn't opened myself in years, trusting the tick of the heart. I'd kept it for so long that I knew I'd have lost my deposit, but I hadn't wanted to return it, to lose the image of Grace coiled in the centre of it.

I slid out from under Grace. She mumbled half awake, then quietened when I slipped a cushion in under the heat of her skull. I tiptoed into the bathroom and opened the rusted hinges of my chest.

The heart was dusty and tarnished and utterly empty. In the centre of it was no picture of Grace, no strands of her hair, no shine of memories, no declarations. The rusting metal squealed when I pulled it out.

UNDERSKIRTS

She found me with my hands around chickens, fingers stretched wide, thumbs over beaks. My skirt, mud-weighed, tugged at my ankles as I dipped low. Silly to curtsey while armed with birds, I knew, but it had to be done. If I'd let go they'd've flown at her, chuttering through her red hair. And what a sight that would've been! The lady, still horsed, with her legs one on either side and her skirt hitching up to show a handspan of stocking. And her horse as white as cuckoo flowers, with its little red haunch-spot not quite hidden by the bridle. I kept my thumbs tight over those dangerous beaks.

So there I was, tangle-skirted and chicken-full, and I'll never know what she saw in me then. Enough, any case, to offer coins to my father – bags full of glinting, enough to make his moustache disappear into the folds of his lips. For my mother, it was the title. Lady's Maid. Fine fetters for the youngest of eight, last to leave. No word from my siblings for years, long gone as they were – the last we saw was the hellfire from their heels across the tops of the hills. And my betrothed, he of the thick knuckles and pale gold hair? The transparent boy who tumbled me across hay, who licked at my earlobes and stickied my palms? I forgot him within a day.

I'll never know what My Lady saw in me, but I know what I saw in her. She was a mirror. Mud-weighed and birdhanded as I was, she still knew me. She knew the things I had been thinking, down deep between my lacings, under the wooden heels of my shoes. The words I shaped with straw before kicking away: she knew them. We were tied as sisters, cousins, lovers. This link between us is a red silk ribbon, a fine silver chain, a length of daisies punched together. It's the loveliest thing I ever saw.

THE HOUSEKEEPER

I'll not be taking part in mistress's activities, oh no. She brings the girls up to the house and that is as it is, but I'll have none of it. She's a fancy lady, no doubt. But even fancy ladies don't need a dozen handmaids, and them changing every few weeks to a new crop of girls. It's to the end that I can't even remember their names, not a one, not a single one. Just a *you there* will suffice for that sort of girl, to my mind.

Such harlotry in their little looks! Mouths round and red like quims, and their bodices low as anything. The mistress must pick out the stitches before she gives the girls the dresses, mark you. No proper dressmaker would make a lady look such a pinchcock.

The first maid was fine enough – mistress did need help with her dressing and suchlike, and her red cheeks and brown hair looked regular enough to fit in at the house. For a while she tied mistress's corsets and arranged mistress's hair, and I kept firm out of their way. Plenty to keep me busy kitchen-side. But I couldn't pretend I didn't see what mistress was about. Tip-tapping through the back corridors where she'd no business to be, flipping up skirts and losing her rings inside girls. Mistress parading those wagtails thinking it was like to tempt me, thinking I was like to be kept feverish at nights with thinking of their ways, that I was like to be some dirty tom. And me with my eyes on the floor like I'm meant! They'll go to the devil, the lot of them. I've got two eyes; how long can I pretend I don't see?

THE LADY

Oh, how I have loved. My days are flaxen and holy with love. My nights are viscous, lucid, spilling over. My finger pads hum. The roots of my hair feel gold-dipped; the meat of my eyes is speckled with gold; gold dust blows across my cheeks. The girls, the girls, and their love. No need for sleep when their saliva is sustenance. Their sweet country cunts and their kiss.

I find them, I whisper of my home, and they're up on my horse before the daisies close. The look in their eyes is clean as dawn. Their fingers in my mouth taste of buttermilk. My castle is a mother, is a lover. Once upon a time, I say, and they follow my hooves inside the walls, and I close the door up tight behind them.

My enchantments keep them for a turn of the sun or a phase of the moon, and then they find the chink in the walls and slip out faster than smoke. I know they look back. I see the light glint off their eyes.

Some do stay; one or two starbellied and honeyfed girls. I tuck them under my swan wing and tickle them close, close enough to share heat. They love love as I do. They see the straight line of my jaw along the length of their thighs and they see how it fits, the geometry of bodies. They have wondered for so long why nothing ever fits, why the knobs of their spines press hard on chairbacks and why they can't lie parallel in bed, and then there I am. I know how to fill the gaps in a girl.

THE DINNER GUEST

She wanted us to know. She's proud of it, I'm sure. The strumpet. The slippering little . . . but let me tell you. You will see.

Two dozen guests for dinner and it was out with the partridge tongues and the songbird hearts in cages of ribs, along with wine sweet enough to pickle kittens. How the ladies cooed! Codswallop, I say. But the ladies like their food to sing.

Three courses in and we were a maid down. I knew because she was a comely thing, applecheeked and apple-breasted, with a glint in her eye like she well knew the parts of a man. I'd been devouring her charms between sips of the lamb-blood soup, and then – gone! For moments I frowned my way around the room, as surely even the most coddled maid would never dare abandon her post mid-meal. And then my eye's wanderings noticed how the lady of the house shifted in her seat! No soup ever caused such moans from a throat, and yet the lady was purring like a pussycat. Seated opposite the lady, I had an artist's perspective; full frontal, so to speak, perfect for observing that actress's change in expression. Shifting my feet under the table, I knew the shape of a body; even through the soles of my shoes I could feel it was that applerumped maid. And the lady moaned, and the lady wriggled; and all the other ladies peered into their soup and began moaning around their spoons.

Such soup, they cried! Such flavours! Bravo!

All the ladies were shifting and groaning, rocking in their seats like they had pigs rutting away at them. You'd have thought it was the greatest soup ever to have been swallowed.

By the bottom of their bowls, the lady was smiling wider than a dagger's blade. The maid was back in her place, her lips plump and wet as a rose after the rain.

And so you see! That grinning tart put on quite a show for me. I know it was for me, because all that ladies do is for the eyes of gentlemen. And I do look forward to seeing more of that lady.

Girl #6

I stayed for a year. I was not the only one – it was three to a bed in My Lady's chamber – but still I stayed. I don't know what I was searching for. I don't know if I found it.

Living in that house was like living inside a painting – one of those lush, dark oil paintings: a still life of over-ripe fruit, a severed boar's head, and a cat toying with a pitted wheel of cheese. Everywhere I went, I was sure people could smell the sweetsalt fleshness on my fingers. Men in the street stopped to stare, stopped to lick their lips, though I was shoulder-to-ankle in my cloak. Her scent went that deep: right under my flesh, all the way to the marrow. For months after I left, I would still catch the breeze of her when I angled my body just the right way. There were creases and edges of me that I just could not get to, and that is where she hid: too far down to scrub out.

My parents knew, somehow. They could smell the shreds My Lady left in me. I went back to the muck of the kitchen and the heat of the stables, but there was no good to be found. Everything was overlaid and underpinned with her. My dresses would not fit: they were too tight, too low, however much fabric I added on. My scarf would not cover my hair, and tendrils slipped out to frame my rosy cheeks. My mouth felt always swollen, always reddened.

I married – a cutout man, all hands and knees – and I stood wide-eyed as a nun in my white dress, calm as can be, like ice would stay cool in my palms. I imagined My Lady when I vowed, thought of how she would glitter and cackle to see her bedfellow in snow-coloured chiffon. I thought my vows would topple her, but she clambered up on them. She strung each word and wore them as a necklace, warming them like pearls.

I never knew what hate and love meant before My Lady.

THE LORD

What makes a woman is a performance of duty, and my wife has long been womanised. I saw well enough to that. From the day I flung her across my pommel to the band of gold, to the hanging of the bloodied sheet to the clockwork of the household, she is a daughter of Eve through and through. Each duty is performed admirably: she whips servants with a firm wrist, she wears her dresses better than a mannequin, and she moans louder than the priciest whore. Her mask will never slip. I do not need to see her to know that.

I dress for her dinners, do I not?

I pay gold for her trousseau, do I not?

I let her take on whichever little maidens she likes, do I not?

That is what makes me a man. I do what needs to be done. I do it fast and I do it well, and no rabbit was ever safe from my arrows.

That is her desire: a man as straight and solid as a wall for her to lean on. A woman's world is the size of the distance from the bedroom to the kitchen. What is she without me? She is unmanned, an empty case. A woman is an actress, and the only thing keeping her on stage is the width of her smile.

I am born a man. I do not need to perform.

THE DAUGHTER

Yes, I told. My father deserved to know. He's a devil with a clefted chin, but he still needed to know about my mother's wickedness because it just was not right. It was not holy. The path to glory is not paved with swooning girls, and no one ever found grace between two legs. So I told and I told and afterwards I glowed for days.

God knew about my mother's sins and my father is the God of this house, so he should have known too. It was my duty, that is all, and it did not matter about my own scuttering feelings or how many times I caught the flash of bare shoulders through the keyhole because it was not about that. It was about staying good. It was about grace, and keeping my own white heels straight on the shining path to heaven. My mother's own feet were no good for that path, after her grubbing in the dirt like that, ingraining those maids onto her flesh. Such things cannot be cleansed and there are no dirty feet in heaven. There is no jealousy in heaven and there was no jealousy in my heart over those girls. They were welcome to my mother. She was a pitcher full of filth with her mouth full of blood and I did not want her attention. I did not want it.

My glow was not from the deed of my telling, understand. It was from the knowledge of God, deep inside me the knowing of all His glory, His radiance warming me through the dark of night. It was grace shining out of me.

THE FRIEND

I attended their house for dinner, the same as a dozen other lords and ladies. I expected an elegant meal – rabbit tongues, perhaps, or eels' eyes – and wine in five different colours. The lady served all my expectations, and her conversation was characteristically delightful – all scandals and intrigues with veiled names. She laughed and touched my hand at all the right moments and, like a fool, I was charmed. Me, in a gown with patched underskirts, and my jewellery only paste – I was the one the lady wanted! No man ever seduced with such confidence. Her smile was as warm as fresh-baked bread, but her eyes were sharp at the corners.

I did not expect to become entangled in her activities. But I tell you; no one could have resisted the lady. After dinner the gentlemen slumped off for cigars and brandy, and the ladies fluttered to the sitting room for champagne. It was not usual for ladies to have so many drinks – it does go to one's head, and as every lady is told, there is not much in her head to absorb all that alcohol. It sloshes about in the space. That must be why I was fooled as I was – it must be!

One by one, the gentlemen visited our sitting room and held out their hands for their ladies. One by one, the ladies flitted out. The room was sotted with champagne and the walls were undulating – I swear they were, the lady is a magician! – and then it was just me and the lady, and then the sitting room became the lady's chambers. The girls' hands were soft as the insides of furs. Their laughter was church bells and their kisses; oh, their kisses. I had never known it could be such a way.

Our discarded skirts were piled high as a church steeple and our throats hummed with lust and we felt honey flow from our bodies, and finally the lady sat at the peak of a tangle of girl-limbs and surveyed her kingdom, when in walked the Lord.

The Girls' Mothers

We knew. From the start, we knew. But we knew too what our girls were. This world is a cold and rutted place for those with brows raised above the horizon.

A handful of shiny circles and these girls are tied to any neat-shoed lady, like or not – but we liked it fine, shame to confess. We liked the words of this Lady and the promise of ever after. The love of a mother for her child is stronger than tides, but we know that the best way for a child is to put one foot in front of the other. Half of a woman is given away each time we split ourselves with child, until all we cradle at night is a scrap of soul. The Lady was a shining road, flat and straight enough for our girls, and she would lead them into the dawn. Our girls had always had itching feet, after all. So we took the coins and we took the promises, but they did not fill the space our girls left.

At nights we pushed with all our breath to hear the thoughts of our girls, but even the harness of daughter to mother can be severed if the walls are thick enough. The Lady's walls were thicker than muscle, and we could not break through. We made believe that our girls smiled like they always had strawberries in their cheeks, and that their shoes were silky as a pigeon's neck feathers. We were not the stepmothers from fairy tales. We did what we thought was best.

We knew what the Lady was, but we liked her ship-wreck-quick smile and the shine on her shoes. We liked her white horse with its one red spot. That horse was just like our girls, we knew, and no amount of whitewash can cover that red dot.

THE ABBOT

It is easy to understand why a lady would wish to escape. We all tire of this earthly plain before long. The way out is grace, and glory exists inside all of us.

The entry into heaven cannot be rushed, and for the lady it will be as slow as she needs it to be. The duty of an anchoress is no easy one, we know that well enough. The contemplation of the grave is perhaps the most difficult, but the lady has as much time as God has granted her. She is young yet, and there will be many years for her to appreciate the gifts of her enclosure. She will find peace in solitude, I am sure.

Her husband has assured me that the lady has craved bare walls and silenced voices for many a year. The lady is fortunate indeed that her husband is willing to sacrifice his wife for her own good. It cannot be easy for him to run a household of women alone, but he is a good man to think only of his dear wife, and I am sure that God will reward him.

The lady's enclosure begins this evening, and I must prepare. The road to heaven is a pebbled one, and she will need a firm hand to steer her through. The contemplation of darkness will help her better than the touch of a hand ever could. Of this, I am sure.

The Lady

My skin hums with it. My flaxenbelly and my moonsmoke, and there are holes, there are holes in me through which the love escapes. The men are men and they are hard, there are no summits to them, nothing to climb up or slip down. My fingers fit into the gaps between the bricks. The moon is the size of my eye. The buttermilk and the daisies, the redness inside cheeks and within the holiest of holies, within the edges of a girl, and this is grace, and this is glory.

A SKULK OF SAINTS

Lauren and Hope live out by the water in a caravan adrift in a field of yellowed grass. The field fills the gap between an abandoned petrol station and an old house converted into a discount tile shop. No one comes near the caravan. Even the tile shop employees skirt the grass, keeping to the path.

In the mornings, Lauren makes a mug of Nescafé, pulls on a fleece, and sits on the flimsy corrugated step of the caravan. It's summer, but the air has a pre-dawn chill, and her fingers ache against the ceramic. Across the water the sun is staining the clouds. She watches the bridge, the steady lines of commuters, her eyes flicking as she sips. If the wind is blowing the right way, she lights up a Marlboro and smokes it as fast as she breathes. Afterwards she tucks the butt under the caravan's sagging belly.

She makes tea – soy milk, two sugars – then sits cross-legged on the bed and strokes Hope's hair until she wakes.

Morning, says Hope, turning the word into a smile.

When Hope has propped herself on the pillows, Lauren presses a kiss to her mouth and hands her the tea. Hope tugs open the curtains. The window doesn't face the water; instead it frames the crows scattered across the field and the ruined church up on the hill and the pylons against the clouds.

You'll be late, says Hope, but Lauren's ear is pressed to

the swell of Hope's middle. She's so far gone that they're almost eye-to-eye, and Lauren is sure that she can feel the press of miniature toes even through the duvet.

She turns her head, finds a strip of skin between the duvet and Hope's nightdress. *Worth it*, she whispers into Hope's bellybutton. She kisses down the mound until she reaches the pink-white scar. She hesitates, begins to kiss along the bumped line. Stops when she realises that Hope has tensed into stillness. Sits up and covers the scar, careful not to knock the arm holding the tea. Kisses instead the safety of Hope's mouth, cheeks, closed eyelids.

Lauren potters around the caravan, opening and closing cupboards until Hope lies back down and closes her eyes. On her way out, she tips the leftover tea onto the yellowed grass then stows the teacup in the glove compartment, cushioned by a bundle of Hope's T-shirts.

There is dew on the leather circle of the steering wheel; Lauren pats it with her sleeve as she turns the ignition key. The Fiat's radio coughs. She taps it off before it starts shouting music, then bumps across the field and onto the bridge. She's driving away from the sun, and the road in front of her is still blue with dawn.

At the hospital, Lauren scrubs the remnants of cigarette and steering wheel and Hope from her hands. Above the sink she sees Saint Agatha carrying her severed breasts on a platter. Lauren dries her hands and hefts an armful of files to her chest. There are so many that her elbows lock; she presses her chin on the top one to stop it slipping to the floor.

Lauren spends the day peering at the insides of people, the evidence of life.

Are you wearing any other jewellery? she asks.

And *Do you have any tattoos?*

And *A hearing aid?*

And *Any surgical staples, pins, screws, plates?*

The patients say things and she ticks the box on the form. Sometimes they nod or shake their heads without a sound, like shy children, and Lauren has to look up after each question to check the answer. Beside the machine she sees Saint Julitta tied to a stake with her flesh charring.

The machine can pull out the tattoo ink, says Lauren.

And *Your piercings might heat up a little.*

And *Metal workers have tiny flecks of metal in their eyes; the machine can pull them out too and then their eyes bleed.*

Lauren does not think this has ever happened, and she only tells it to younger patients who want scary stories. Even then, she only tells it to the ones who aren't really ill. Broken bones are fine. The ones with shaking hands and threadveined skin don't need horror stories.

With every image of bone and brain, sinus and intestine, Lauren wishes she could see the insides of Hope. Laid out like this, clean and simple. No mystery and no questions. People are more than DNA, she knows, but if she could feel their child from her insides, know him with her own flesh the way that Hope does, it would be better. It would make sense. He would feel more like her own; he would be more than just an idea.

She can't shake the nag that Hope knows something that she does not, some mothering secret that makes other women nod at one another knowingly in the baby-food aisle. Lauren is tired of being on the outside.

At the end of her shift, she taps her foot on the pedal of the bin, ready to drop in the waste. The white metal lid flips up, making the lips of the yellow bag inside puff towards her. It's almost full: discarded sharps and blood-bloomed cotton. Insides, outside. She drops in the waste.

On the way home, Lauren practices saying *The thing is, Hope. Listen, Hope, it's this thing. Hope, this is the thing.* But she cannot finish, because she does not know what the thing is. It's an ache of being stuck on the outside; at a distance from their child, hidden and unreal. These are the things, but she cannot fit them into words, and so it is hard to finish the sentence.

She's driving away from the sun again; in the rear-view she sees the buttery light and the bone-white turbines lined up along the horizon.

She turns off the road before she gets to the field. The car hums along fresh-laid tarmac and she checks off the street names: Glenview, Rowanwood, Oaklands. There is no forest for miles, just pylons and turbines. Lauren counts up to 23 Cedarpark Road then idles outside, imagining the windows lit and the bare rooms warm as a cocoon. No one has ever lived in the house; its insides will still smell of paint and air-freshener.

She scoops up the contents of the glove compartment and walks to the door. Posts Hope's T-shirts one by one through the letterbox. Imagines them crowning the pile on the inside of the door: nail clippers and wooden spoons and lipsticks and earrings and socks. The mug will not fit through the slot, so she stands it at the side of the door, upside down so it won't fill with rain.

She gets back in the car and turns towards the field. The SOLD sticker on the board outside the house is beginning to curl up at the edges.

For dinner, Hope makes boiled haddock and minted

couscous. She cuts the mint with a blade in the shape of a half moon with a handle at each end; she waits until Lauren gets home to do this because they both like the smell. Lauren sits on the corrugated step, beer bottle dangling from one hand, and watches the sway of Hope's shoulders as she rocks the blade. The moon is as thin as a smile.

Lauren says:

I went by the house.

And *Everything was signed months ago.*

And *No arguments. I'll pack.*

Hope says:

This is our house.

And *I will not leave.*

And finally, hand on her belly, *If there's space for him in there, there's space for us in here.*

Later in bed, sleep velvet-heavy behind Lauren's eyes, she folds herself into Hope's side. She slips her hand under Hope's nightdress. Presses her palm to the scar. Keeps it there, even after the tense of muscles.

You don't have to be scared, Hope. This one is coming home with us.

Hope does not reply for a long time – so long that Lauren begins to sink into sleep.

But how can I keep him safe out there?

The first contraction hits when Lauren is sitting on the corrugated step, watching the sun seep into the clouds. She doesn't need to wait for Hope to call out; the tensing of her muscles sends a tiny ripple through the caravan's flesh.

Lauren throws her half-finished Nescafé and Marlboro under the caravan, grabs the overnight bag, circles her fingers around Hope's wrist.

Walking through the hospital's main entrance, with

Hope's grip squeezing tight her hand, Lauren sees Saint Felicity cradling the bones of her seven murdered sons, Saint Margaret of Antioch being swallowed by a dragon, Saint Mary of Oignies cutting off chunks of her own flesh. Then a gasp as a contraction hits and the world shrinks to the size of Hope's body. The inside, even smaller than the outside. This is all there is.

Twelve hours later, they meet their son. He is as red and scrubbed as a Valentine heart.

He is a stranger, but his face is familiar to Lauren, like someone she used to know in childhood. They lie on the hospital bed, bodies curled into brackets, and discover that he fits perfectly into the space between them.

Look at what we made, says Lauren. *Look at what we made from what others didn't need.*

While the rest of her family are asleep, Lauren drives away from the hospital, away from the sun.

In the field, she hooks the caravan onto the tow-bar attached to the bumper. Even with the accelerator almost flat, the car shrieks but does not move. She gets out of the car and puts her shoulder to the caravan's back end, shoving in rhythm to the throb of the cars over the bridge. With a disapproving sound, the caravan's wheels tip forwards out of the dirt. She gets back in the car, presses her foot down, and prays.

Three turns later, Lauren stops in front of the house and pulls a ring of keys from the glove compartment. Inside, the house smells of paint and dust. Unfamiliar.

She scoops up the piles of Hope's belongings from under the letterbox and puts them around the house in their proper places. Goes back outside. Unhooks the caravan in the street in front of their house. Gets back in the car. Turns the key. Drives into the sun.

THE LAST 3,600
SECONDS

When the dog starts barking, we know it's beginning. Or rather, ending.

We grab handfuls of bottles and climb up onto the roof of the house. She stumbles and her foot slips into the gutter sopped with dead leaves. I grab her wrists and pull her clear – sure, she's not the person I'd choose to do this with, but she's my only option so I might as well be nice. Plus I don't want her to drop the vodka.

I can hear the world beginning to shift. Sirens frenzy, streets protest, every animal in the city is whining or screeching or crying. We settle on the roof, backs to the chimney, and secure the bottles between our knees. She's already started on the rum before I manage to arrange my feet on the loosening tiles. I shift closer, our legs pressed, and she drops the rum and stares at me with a look that says *already?* I shake my head – not yet – and move away so there's an inch of air between us.

I can feel everything getting closer, the past catching up. All the cunts and cocks and clits I've ever touched. That guy I sucked off behind the all-night garage; the girl I slowfucked in my sunny kitchen; those sisters I seesawed between for a fortnight, never sure which one I wanted to call my girlfriend, then ended up with neither. I left them all on the other side of the world, and now they're creeping back to me.

Above us, the sky is a hundred colours at once: sunset, sunrise, aurora borealis, clouds and clear blue. It is every sky that has ever existed. The colours are snagged with stars and planets and planes. I figured the planes would have stopped running, but I guess if it's going to end then it might as well end in a metal tube in the sky.

Because it is going to end, and everything I have is not enough. I need another soul, another set of guts to feel this. Maybe her body merging with mine will be the grace I need.

In school they taught us about the Big Bang: the universe expanding out from a dense primordial heat. They didn't tell us that eventually it was all going to contract back again. For a month I'd been planning to tell her that I needed more space, some time to myself. Then they announced that the world was crashing in on our heads, and now all I want is to get inside her.

She's always taken up too much space: big tits, big mouth, always so loud and hot and restless. Wherever I wanted to be, she'd already be there. Brushing our teeth at night, she'd always have her head over the sink when I wanted to spit. She always used the last tea bag and ate the last biscuit and drained the hot-water tank, and it always made me –

It's coming, it's soon, I know it, there's no time left. The dog is chewing his feet and the planes are so close I can see the logos on their tails. Tiny fires have broken out all along the horizon, brighter than the approaching stars. Her leg is touching mine, our knee joints pressing hard, and I throw down the whisky and start sucking on the vodka –

That tendency of hers made the fucking so good, she was

everywhere, all over me at once, and I loved that feeling of her breasts pressed up against my face and her wetness on the sheets and her hands holding me down. I wanted all of her then, and soon I'll be –

Now the world is so loud that I can't hear anything, everything is colours and sound and sky and planes and the burn of alcohol and her body – her body on mine, in mine, skin and bone and sinew merging, and this is it, it's now. We are.

THE BROKEN WEST

Daniel first kisses his brother in a town where no one knows them, a no-account place that's barely even a town, just some buildings clustered around the highway: a smoky bar, an empty motel, a convenience store that only sells candy and condoms and beer. The nearest gas station is twenty miles away. The nearest bus station is fifty.

The trail had gone cold somewhere around Louisville, but now their father's journal is back on track. They know for sure he was in this town, and only a year before he died. They can't be sure whether he's wanted here, but it's possible. Thirty miles up the road there's a bank and a school, and Dad could rarely pass those institutions without some inklings of a crime. If their father was here then, maybe their brother is here now.

Daniel can taste the place on the back of his tongue: beer and peanuts and stale sweat. Shreds of cheatgrass rustle in his boot-treads with every step. He's spent a year checking the face of everyone he passes – does that guy have his eyes, Jack's chin, Dad's ears? The only thing he's discovered is how similar everyone looks. He can't even tell anymore which noses look like his, which foreheads, which hairlines. They're all like his, and yet none are.

Jack climbs onto a barstool, orders a beer and a shot of bourbon. The barman looks at Daniel – the same? – and before Daniel nods he compares the barman's face to Jack's.

Five drinks later, Jack goes to the bathroom. As soon as the bathroom door shuts, Daniel orders three bourbons and necks them, one after the other, swallowing hard so he can't cough them back up. Saliva fills his mouth, and he grips the bar until red train tracks appear on his palms.

The bourbon stays down, and Daniel is still pretending not to notice the guy who followed Jack into the bathroom – scrawny, red-eyed, his leather jacket hanging off his shoulders like he's only bones. Tonight is Jack's turn at the Investigation, though he takes more turns than Daniel because he enjoys it more. Daniel always worries that it'll get too far before he finds out, that the other man will already be inside him before he recognises the shape of his eyes or the angle of his nose. That doesn't seem to bother Jack, and yet he still won't kiss Daniel.

Daniel had tried in Topeka to make Jack feel better after he'd puked up a bottle of whisky. He'd tried in Oklahoma City to distract Jack after he'd been slapped by every waitress in the diner. He'd tried in Little Rock to console Jack after their truck's tyre blew again. Daniel had been shoved away, yelled at, puked on. For Jack, the lost brother is more valuable than the found. Daniel knows it, but it still feels like a sucker-punch.

Daniel's halfway through his next beer when Jack slides back into his barstool, his eyes glazed and his cheeks scraped raw. Daniel can't tell if he's been fighting or fucking, and it doesn't really matter. Faces look different close up, and the only way to get that close to a stranger is to kiss them or choke them. It's just someone else to cross off the list. Someone else they didn't recognise.

At midnight the bar closes, and Daniel steers Jack across the highway to the motel. The road is acned with yellow starthistle and the parking lot is empty except for their pickup, road-dusted and dipped in rust. The motel's flickering floodlights pick out movement: shapes flashing white then grey. Daniel's still squinting his smoke-reddened eyes, trying to combine the shapes into something he knows, when Jack shouts out a curse and launches himself away from Daniel and into the side of the pickup, except that between Jack and the pickup there's that moving shape, and Daniel sees now that it's a person.

Jack's shouting, pressing the person against the pickup, and he's sliding down the door and trying to crawl under the truck, and Jack grabs his ankles and pulls him back out, skin on gravel. And Daniel sees his face and it's just a kid, it's a boy, scrambling and choking, trying to do anything, to be anywhere except here. The kid's saying sorry sorry no please no.

Jack is not listening. He is kicking, punching, screaming. Daniel is grabbing at limbs: Jack's, the kid's, trying to get Jack to stop, but Jack isn't stopping, even when Daniel's sure he knows it's just a kid. Daniel gets in between Jack and the kid, Jack's kicks tangling in his legs but he stays standing, and he holds Jack's jaw with both hands and he kisses him.

And the kid is crying behind them, gravel crunching as he tries to move away, but all Daniel knows is Jack, and it's taking everything in him to hold Jack still and kiss him hard and not cry. Because this is it, it's working, Jack's kissing him back, even as his muscles are tight and his hands are twitching and Daniel can taste the anger in their mouths. This time, in this no-account barely-town, it's happening just right. As right as it can be, at least.

And Jack pushes him away, but the kid has already run across the empty highway, still crying but both legs working, pumping to get him away.

And Daniel can see, even in the flicker of the floodlights, that the kid doesn't look like either of them.

The second time that Daniel kisses his brother is after Jack gets the shit kicked out of him for the third time in a week. Jack lies on his hard motel bed, boots dusting gravel on the blanket, and cries until he chokes. After an hour, he lets Daniel wipe off the blood and the dirt and the dried tears. After two hours, he lets Daniel hold him. After three, he sleeps.

Daniel lies rigid on the single bed, not daring to move in case Jack wakes and pushes him away. His arm is numb under Jack's shoulder and he desperately has to piss, but he does not move. He breathes slowly, filling his lungs with his brother's smell: sweat and whisky and something metallic. He focuses on the paintings of faded green trees hanging crooked on the wall and the dripping sound coming from the bathroom. He can feel the heat of Jack's skin on his cheek.

Tonight's fight had not been part of the Investigation. Someone had tried to steal their truck, and this time it wasn't some punk kid. The guy had left the truck, but not before ramming his extremities into Jack's belly.

A beating was worth saving the truck. Without the truck, they'd never find their brother, and the Investigation would be a failure. All that fucking, all that blood, would be for nothing. Daniel knows it was worth it, but he'd still give anything to make Jack stop hurting.

Daniel slides down on the bed, holding his breath until he's dizzy, hardly daring to move in case he wakes Jack.

Finally his face is level with Jack's, though his feet are now hanging off the edge of the bed. Lying here, he's reminded of how small Jack's bones are.

Daniel inches his body sideways, trying to press as much of it as possible against Jack. They meet at the shins, arms, lips, forehead, and suddenly it's a kiss, sweet and soft. Daniel stays that way for a long time, his body tight against Jack's.

Three weeks later, two states over, another piece-of-shit town. The brothers have moved up in the world: this town has a gas station *and* a diner. Daniel, of course, wants to go to the diner; Jack, of course, stomps wordlessly to the bar. Daniel does not drive the pickup, Daniel does not get the bed by the window, and Daniel does not choose where they go. Daniel knows that this town must have a daytime, but they've been here for fourteen hours and the sky still looks dark. The stench of flowering goldenrod is caught at the back of Daniel's throat.

Their father's journal is hard to follow; it seemed like he'd written a lot of it drunk, or in a moving car. Daniel and Jack don't even know if he's been through this town, but that doesn't stop Daniel peering at each face as they walk through the bar.

The air smells of farms: dirt and the flesh of animals. Jack points at the cheapest bottle and the barman empties it into two glasses. The faces in here are the same as the faces in every dirty bar in every shit town in the whole of this stinking country. The same and not the same.

Daniel hasn't even touched his drink, but he can feel the fumes burning up his nose. Jack's glass is half empty, and he keeps his fist clenched around it between gulps, as if afraid someone will snatch it away before he is done.

Daniel tries to watch Jack out of the corner of his eye, wishing he had hair to hide behind. Jack shaves both their heads monthly – he says it helps to see their bone structure and features, helps to memorise them. It makes their faces easier to compare.

Jack seems intent on his drink, so Daniel slides an inch closer on his barstool. Jack drains his glass and slams it on the bar, the crack gunshot-loud over the droning jukebox. Daniel gets the message, slides two inches away on his stool.

There has been no more kissing. Every morning, Jack undresses, showers, and redresses behind a locked bathroom door. If they could afford it, Daniel is sure that Jack would book separate rooms.

Tonight it is Daniel's turn at the Investigation. He raises his glass, fumes clouding in his throat, then lowers it. Standing by the pool table, in mud-spattered boots and a wrinkled T-shirt, is a man. He pulls his hair back from his face to take a shot, and Daniel sees Jack's nose. The ball thumps into the pocket, and the man smiles: Daniel sees Dad's dimple.

Daniel finishes his drink in three burning gulps, swallowing hard to keep it from rising back up. He fixes his eyes on the man's legs and walks towards him. He pulls a cigarette from the crumpled pack in his pocket, sticks it between his lips, and asks for a light.

Five minutes later they're in the alley behind the bar, the man's face lit by the sickly yellow moon. Daniel pushes him against the wall, stumbling on ground littered with broken planks, smashed bottles, shreds of plastic. The man licks Daniel's neck and Daniel pulls away, holding the man's hair back off his face with both hands, looking for Jack's nose. The man shows his teeth and undoes Daniel's belt.

Daniel stares at the man's face under the dull half-moon, and he knows. He sees himself, his brother, his father.

Daniel stumbles, gets his balance. The man has Daniel's pants down on the uneven ground and Daniel doesn't want it, can't want it, but his body doesn't listen; his body knows that the man smells like Jack, that the man has the shapes and angles of Jack, and his body knows that that is good enough. Daniel leans his head back against the wall and stares up at the moon and feels the spread of the man's saliva across his skin.

Daniel leaves the man on his knees in the alley and goes back into the bar, back to his brother. Jack looks up and raises his eyebrows – is it? – but Daniel just shakes his head. He takes Jack's unsteady arm, slides him off the barstool, and leads him back to the motel.

BIBLIOPHAGY

#1. The Time He Hid The Words In The Footwell Of The Car

He knows that his wife knows. She can smell the adverbs on his tongue in the mornings. But he cannot get through another evening in that house without consonants. His daughter sits in her wardrobe dappling the edge of a razor along her inner arm; the tissues stain the toilet bowl pink. His son blows up airports and builds towns full of women with beachball breasts and men with wings covered in black boils. His wife stutters home from work with arms full of carrier bags and frowns at the tiles he spent all day gluing to the walls of the vestibule: red and blue roses with thorns as big as dragons' teeth. They are the wrong colour. He knows it. She keeps frowning. He says that he will go to the 24-hour hardware shop to get the right tiles and walks down the garden path swinging his keyring around his finger and whistling the theme tune from a TV programme and he drives his car around the block and parks under a sycamore which gently vomits leaves onto the roof and lies down on the back seat and reaches into the footwell and brings up handfuls of words and closes his eyes and swallows them.

#2. THE TIME HE HID THE WORDS AT THE BACK OF THE FRIDGE

In the vegetable drawer. Behind the onions. Far enough past their best that no one will pull them out for spag bol but not old enough to be binned. The words will be safe there, cushioned by the softening onions, silenced by their papery skins. He feigns deep breathing until the moon has settled above the skylight, then slips from under his wife's arm. Standing pigeon-toed and bruise-kneed in the light from the fridge, his neck finally stops twitching. The words are waiting, cold as milk. When he reaches for the words he feels his heels already beginning to rise, already beginning to lift him higher, beginning to move him up up up. He turns away so that the moon is hidden behind next door's chimney. He lifts the words. He shudders to think how smooth the vowels will feel along his oesophagus. He swallows.

#3. THE TIME HE HID THE WORDS IN THE TOES OF HIS DRESS SHOES

It is getting more difficult. His arms are in slings after he fell off the roof trying to talk to the disappearing moon. His children will not hold his gaze. Sometimes he gets up at dawn to go into the woods and take off all his clothes and wait to freeze, but he never makes it past the end of the road. When he gets home his hands shake too much to hold his morning coffee. He loves his children but they are not verbs. They are only pronouns and he is a fragment. He is surrounded by the dregs of words and no matter how many he swallows he cannot focus on the moon. He plants unsteady kisses on his family's foreheads. He climbs the stairs and crawls into his wardrobe. He lifts his shoes and stares at the sickly tangle of consonants. This is the last, he says, and he swallows.

COIN-OPERATED
BOYS

That August, Elodie Selkirk became the latest lady in Paris to order a coin-operated boy. Despite her hooked nose and missing pinkie finger, Elodie was suffering from a rash of suitors; unfortunately for them, she was in no need of a gentleman. Elodie glanced down the hall to make sure that the maid was still safely in her room, as instructed – it was best to keep the boy a secret until she could check him over. She straightened the silk bow at her throat and opened the door.

Her basement apartment was close to the busiest shopping street in Paris, and all of the city's ephemera were passing by, their feet at her eye-level. A parade of life, from the glittering right down to the groaning: whispering petticoats dirtied at the hem, leather shoes shinier than pennies, wheels ticking on cobblestones, snatches of scandal . . . Usually, Elodie could not stand the racket, but it all slipped out of focus the moment she saw the boy. From the calm angles of his cheeks to the ruled lines of his cravat, the boy was a mathematical sum. He added up perfectly.

Mademoiselle Selkirk? I am pleased to meet you. His

voice was as clean as dew, but Elodie would not forget her manners.

Do come in, sir. There is tea in the parlour. She swept her arm to clarify, fingers carefully curled to hide the missing pinkie. The boy bowed as he passed her. His pinstriped boater seemed to tilt; Elodie looked away from the imperfection as she closed the door, and by the time she walked to the parlour he was sitting at a perfect right angle to the chaise longue.

She seated herself opposite him and poured the tea. She had not made the tea, of course; the maid had been instructed to set the scene, then disappear to the kitchen. The boy was Elodie's personal business. That staff did not need to see him.

What is your name, sir?

The boy stirred sugar into his tea, then pushed the cup away.

Is it . . . Elodie considered. *Luc-Pierre?*

The boy smiled, revealing teeth as white as salt. *My name is Luc-Pierre,* he said.

And you may call me Elodie. As long as no one can hear, that is.

The boy – Luc-Pierre, she thought with a smile – nodded an assent. Elodie sipped at her tea. She would dismiss the maid early and turn down Luc-Pierre's bed herself. Only Elodie could get the sheets neat enough, and now that Luc-Pierre was here everything must be perfect.

Elodie's need for a boy had been sparked by one suitor in particular, Claude di Haviland, who would not take a blush as a refusal. He'd left his calling card ten times a day, finally driven by Elodie's silence to wail her name along the alleyways in the starlit hours. Wrapped in a clumsily-buttoned overcoat and clutching a rose to overpower the stench from the Seine, Elodie had crept up the stairs from her basement apartment and tried to shush him. She was not at all prepared for such a situation and her hushing was ineffectual at best. Soon his wails encouraged a chorus from the neighbourhood cats: they lined up along the wall behind him, tails flicking like conductors' batons. When Elodie's neighbours had begun ignoring her in the marketplace, tutting about their interrupted dreams and awakened babies, Elodie knew something had to be done.

The day after the coin-operated boy arrived, Claude came calling once more. Elodie dismissed the maid and swung the door wide herself. In his surprise Claude forgot to remove his hat, and sat on the couch in all his outdoor clothes. It was so rude that Elodie had to avert her eyes while pouring the tea, but she still remembered to provide a silver pot of sugar.

My dear Claude, whispered Elodie. *Have you met Luc-Pierre?*

At that moment, just as he had been instructed, Luc-Pierre swept into the room and took a seat next to Elodie. Their knees were almost touching, and Elodie's heart beat so hard she feared it would rattle the whalebone of her corset.

Charmed, choked out Claude. As the co-owner of A Boy For All Seasons, with his sister Nora, he would well know the function of coin-operated boys. The boy's presence was as clear a spurning as any lady could provide. Claude managed two sips of his tea before making his excuses, and the neighbourhood cats lost a choir member.

The next week, Elodie went walking along the Seine with Luc-Pierre. She had stuffed his buttonhole with three fat yellow roses, which she knew was a little excessive; he did not have the ability to smell, but she still did not want the reek of the polluted river to upset him. She placed a handful of the yellow roses along her hat brim so that they matched. It was the perfect time for a walk: the streets were freshly swept and the morning sun had not yet begun to burn their eyes. Elodie felt her skin prickle with perspiration and slowed her pace. They were young lovers out for a stroll, and there was no reason in the world to rush.

Would you care for an ice, sir? Elodie nudged her fingers on Luc-Pierre's arm as she spoke: the affection was daring for such a public place, but she could not resist. In return, Luc-Pierre graced her with a smile.

I confess I do not know, mademoiselle. Would you care for one?

For the first time in her life, Elodie made a sound that could be described as a giggle. *Oh, do let us be wicked. One ice each! Look, the cart is just over there.*

She steered him past a cluster of petal-coloured parasols, which presumably had ladies underneath.

Good sir, husked a voice. Elodie and Luc-Pierre turned to see a woman in patched and lurid silks, one arm outstretched towards them. *Might you wish to accompany one of your fellows on a jaunt?* The woman spoke with a mocking undertone, and was looking at Luc-Pierre as if Elodie were invisible. A horde of tabby cats purred circles around the woman's feet.

No thank you, mademoiselle, said Luc-Pierre neatly.

More coins if you're with me. Three is the fashion now, sir.

And then, dear Reader, the wretch dared to wink at the promenading couple! Elodie clenched her teeth tight together, almost choking on her revulsion. She let go of Luc-Pierre's arm and stepped close to the woman. She spoke in a voice between a whisper and a murmur, safe in the knowledge that her voice was drowned out by the clatter of hooves and shouts of the street-sellers and the torrent of unspoken rage and lust and frustration roaring between everybody's ears.

Madame, I would not expect you to observe the difference between your own putrid clockwork and the perfect mathematics of this gentleman. Now take this – Elodie pressed a trio of coins into the woman's palm – *and ensure that you never bother us again.*

In a moment, Elodie's back was to the woman and her gloved hand was once more resting on Luc-Pierre's capable arm. She selected red ices, as they matched her beau's suit-jacket admirably well.

That very day, Claude had deigned to rise before midday to help out in A Boy For All Seasons. Resting between deliveries, he spotted Elodie and her beau strolling in perfect sync with their heads tilted together. He recognised his own stock, but that did not stop the jealousy from burning up his throat.

Claude's foot somehow ended up at the edge of the kerb just as Luc-Pierre passed; coin-operated boys become unstable when not at right angles, as Claude well knew, and he only just managed to catch poor Elodie as Luc-Pierre toppled into the gutter.

Oh, my love! she cried, breaking free from Claude's grasp to bend over Luc-Pierre. Claude could not fail to miss her choice of words, and it was this that made him skulk back to bed and refuse to help in the shop for the rest of the week. Elodie took Luc-Pierre home and fixed him up as well as she was able, feeling sick with guilt.

And that is how Elodie got her coin-operated boy, and

how Claude's jealousy was fired, and how this whole sorry tale began to unfold.

∽

He kept an assortment of thimble-sized people in a snuff box in his top pocket, but that is not why he was unsuitable, said Cara O'Donohue, pinching her fork delicately between thumb and forefinger. She then rather ruined the effort by using it to lift an obscenely large mouthful of cake. Cara is not her real name, of course, but we must protect her reputation in case she reads this.

How simply dreadful, Elodie murmured, averting her eyes while trying to look sympathetic.

You have no idea, ma chérie! Cara rearranged the row of lilac frills below her décolleté. *His moustaches were never waxed. Never! Well, perhaps once.*

Goodness, said Elodie, though of course she had stopped listening by now. These fortune-telling sessions were usually simple enough – new thrills are on the horizon, charming strangers admire you from afar, beware gentleman with tarnished watch-chains – but Cara did not seem to really want her fortune told. She wanted a captive audience, and she was willing to pay for it.

Tongue for luncheon! And on a Friday. Quite unthinkable, I'm sure you agree, chirped Cara.

Oh, when would she hush? This was Elodie's final afternoon with Luc-Pierre, and Cara's incessant chatter was spoiling it. Their weeks together were the most wonderful of Elodie's life and she could not bear to think that it was almost over.

She risked a glance out of the café's front window. Luc-Pierre sat just where she had left him, an untouched cup on the table. His pinstriped boater was tilted to the left, and she ached to adjust it for him. Then again, it was best for him not to appear too dapper; already he was getting many an admiring glance from the other ladies, and if one of them were to proposition him then he would jaunt off with them. Poor boy, he did not know any better. It was deep in the cogs of his being. He needed Elodie, she was sure.

Don't you agree, ma chérie? asked Cara, reaching for another mini-pâtisserie. From her tone, Elodie surmised that this was not the first time the question had been asked.

Oh, indeed, she breezed. *I quite agree. Now, let us return to the fates. I feel that they . . . that they . . . oh, goodness me!*

Elodie swooned back in her chair as if overcome by the chatter of spirits. As Cara fussed, Elodie risked another glance through the window. Luc-Pierre had not moved at all. For a moment she worried that his clockwork had run down – but she had fed him with two-dozen coins last night, and Nora had reassured her that each coin was good for two hours of even the most vigorous movements. Those two-dozen coins were worth it for the pleasures of Luc-Pierre's company, no doubt about that – but they led to Elodie sitting here, being bored to tears by Cara O'Donohue. She coughed and blinked back to life, trying not to sneeze at the stench of violets wafting from the handkerchief Cara was dabbing at her cheeks.

My dear, whispered Elodie, *the fates have spoken. They are very pleased with you, and they have good news. They wish me to tell you that there is a pleasant surprise on the horizon. Very pleasant indeed.* Elodie leaned forwards conspiratorially; Cara leaned forwards too, so that their powdered foreheads almost touched across the table. *The surprise involves a certain gentleman.*

Cara squealed. *Monsieur di Haviland?*

Elodie felt a twinge in her chest at Claude's name, but recovered quickly. *The spirits cannot name individuals, you understand. They mention a straight back, shiny hair, a chivalrous manner –*

But that must be Monsieur di Haviland! He is so very knightly and he walks with his back pointing straight to heaven.

Elodie smiled, fancying that she heard her cheeks creak at the effort. *How astute you are. It must be that very gentleman.*

Cara primped at her dark ringlets so they framed her cheeks, glancing over her shoulder into the crowd as if the fates were going to deliver Claude di Haviland at any moment. Well, thought Elodie, perhaps they would. He was probably the only man left in Paris whom Cara had not yet terrified away. Claude was unexpected and boisterous and his garments always lay at all sorts of raucous angles. He would not do at all. And yet, there was something about the twitch of his smile and the way he had caught her just before she tripped . . .

Through the café's window, Elodie caught a glimpse of Luc-Pierre's perfectly-pointed chin. No, Claude di Haviland would not do at all. But now that he had stopped calling on Elodie, perhaps Cara's fortune would indeed come true. And ducks might fly to the moon.

This has been wonderful, dear Elodie, said Cara, already bustling to her feet. *But I simply must dash. You provided fresh insights into my life and future, as always, and I thank you for that. I can't think what I would do without you. You really are a wonderful friend.* She tucked a fabric pouch of coins under Elodie's napkin, fussed once more at her curls, and disappeared into the crowd.

Elodie took a moment to collect her thoughts – did Cara really consider them friends? did she pay all her friends for their company? what was the slowest possible route she could take to A Boy For All Seasons? – then walked out of the café. It was time to return Luc-Pierre.

From the outside, the true nature of A Boy For All Seasons was not clear. Nestled between a milliner and an academic bookshop, both aimed at those with outsize heads, the building appeared to be a rather dingy men's clothing shop. The only unusual aspect was that the shop's name was in a pale pink font with silvered edges: a colour combination designed to discourage gentlemen from entering. Occasionally a lady may enter looking for a snuff box or pair of gloves for her husband, but most customers knew exactly what they wanted. And they always got it.

When Elodie and Luc-Pierre pushed open the door of A Boy For All Seasons, Nora was neatening the display of cravats. Her waistcoat was neatly fastened, the buttons shined and the hems starched. Her dark hair was tucked up under her velvet pork-pie hat and her trousers were loose enough to maintain the illusion. She was the very picture of a competent shopkeeper, and she played the role well. The customers did not wish to feel that they were purchasing flesh in a seedy back parlour, after all; the boys were officially meant as companions, and their purpose was simply to discourage over-enthusiastic beaus. At least, that is what Nora stated whenever the lawman came calling.

Elodie! And Luc-Pierre. What a fine twosome you make.

You are wicked. Do not tease me so.

I do not tease. You are fine indeed, and I very much hope that you will find your own Luc-Pierre. One without a little stand in a little shop, that is. Nora busied herself with straightening

Luc-Pierre's hat and neatening his collar, and Elodie could not keep the pained look from her face.

Elodie looked down at her boots. *I know I should not ask, dear Nora, but I must. Luc-Pierre, has he ... I mean, is he ... booked?*

No, I shall let him rest. There is a waiting list for him, of course, but he can stay here for a day while I get him fixed up. Nora sighed and tipped back the rim of her pork-pie hat. *And I must stay in any case to mind the shop. I shall send Claude with the deliveries. But oh, damn him! He is worth less than the mud on my boots. Still in bed, no doubt, sleeping off the effects of the midweek revelries.* She took Luc-Pierre's hand and led him into the back room, calling back to Elodie: *One moment, my dear, and we'll have your coins back!*

Oh, you really don't have to – just because we're friends, you mustn't give me any special treatment, you know ... Elodie peered into the back room, tugging at the fingers of her gloves. *Nora, do you need my help? Just to make sure that Luc-Pierre is comfortable. He is so used to my presence, you know ...* She trotted after them.

Claude de Haviland was not still in bed; quite the opposite. He had lurked beneath his bedcovers until he heard his sister slamming the front door to go downstairs to the shop, then swept off the blankets and leapt to his feet. Well, perhaps he dozed for a brief hour or two before he rose. But when he did rise, it was with the excitement of a devil.

His motivation? Love! Love was the only emotion that could stir his limbs and whip up his heart. Love, oh love! And Claude knew how love felt.

Even crouched over with a drinking glass pressed to the floorboards, Claude still made sure to keep a brooding look on his face. He knew it was effective – Cara O'Donohue's desperate giggles told him as much – and he wanted to be ready in case Mme. Selkirk had a reason to come to his room. He'd have a bit of a job explaining why he was on his knees listening at the boards, but she'd soon forgive him when she noticed the tenderness in his chocolate-brown eyes. Ladies always forgave Claude di Haviland. Except, alas, for Mme. Selkirk: the one lady he wanted, and the only one who would not have him.

The problem was that the drinking glass was not a gramophone trumpet, and the most he could hear from downstairs was the shuffle of shoes and the occasional high-pitched laugh. He knew that Mme. Selkirk was down-stairs – even in his head he could not call her Elodie, not even his one true love – because he had seen her approach the house from his window. And her hand clasped in that of the filthy automaton.

Well, Claude had something that the clutch of clockwork never would: a plan. If he could not make Mme. Selkirk love him as he was, then he would become something that she *could* love. Tossing the glass aside, he reached for a pin-stripe boater, a pair of compasses, and a scalpel.

Autumn was looming, bright with the rain of dead leaves and raucous with the last gasps of summer lovers. Every hat-brim bloomed with slightly wilted roses, every shoe was adorned with buckles gleaming brighter than the sun. And over it all, the reek of the Seine – but let's not mind that, for you may buy a sweet-smelling posy at any street corner.

For Elodie, September smelled sour with loss. Since losing Luc-Pierre, she could not eat. She could not sleep.

She snapped at her maid for forgetting to polish the sugar-spoon, for opening the door too vigorously, for scuffing her feet as she walked. Lying wide-eyed in the insomniac moonlight, she realised that she even missed the wails of Claude di Haviland and his feline choir.

After several weeks of mooning around the city, both hoping and fearing to spot Luc-Pierre on the arm of another lady, Elodie decided that enough was enough. Nora was her best friend and would surely understand. She would march into A Boy For All Seasons with her fists full of coins, if that was what it would take.

When the maid announced Mme. di Haviland before breakfast was even on the table, Elodie was so surprised that she had nodded without thinking. She tried to smooth the frown from between her brows so as not to insult her friend.

My dear, what a pleasant . . . Elodie began, her words failing at the look on Nora's face. *But what is wrong?*

Nora's jaw was clenched so hard that her lips had turned white. She did not remove her velvet pork-pie hat or sit on the chaise-longue. *You must come now. There is no time to wait. Claude, he* . . . *I thought he was working on the repairs to a boy, you know, so I left him to it. For weeks and weeks, Elodie! I just let him do it. I could not know! And now, he* . . . Standing in the dimly-lit doorway, Nora seemed lumines-cent with panic. *You will see for yourself. But you must come. Please, Elodie.*

Without waiting, Nora stepped back into the hallway and opened the door herself. It was all Elodie could do to pull on her hat and coat before Nora bustled off down the street.

Elodie had not managed to keep pace, so by the time she

arrived at A Boy For All Seasons the door was wide open and Nora was nowhere to be seen.

Mme. di Haviland? Elodie called as she stepped into the shop. Her gaze swept from left to right: past the polished glass of the counter, the closed door of the back room, the shoes and cravats and handkerchiefs in a dozen shades of blue. In the corner of the darkened shop Luc-Pierre slouched, picking at the skin around his thumbnail. He was hatless and the edge of his shirt was untucked.

In her surprise, Elodie cried out before she knew what she was saying. *Luc-Pierre! You look so . . .* Imperfect. Awkward. Repulsive. . . . *different.*

It was not until he approached her that she realised what was wrong. There was a depth to his gaze and a roll to his walk that was out of character, and yet utterly familiar. With a jolt that pressed all the air from her lungs, Elodie realised why she recognised his manner. He was a *man* – just like the dozens, hundreds, thousands of other men peacocking messily around the streets of Paris. She wilted to her knees on the floor.

Elodie, called Nora from the back room.

Elodie stumbled to her feet and walked through the door to the back room. There, perched neatly on the edge of a chair, was Claude. His cravat was ruler-straight and his eyes shone flat as a pond in summer.

Good morning, Mme. Selkirk, said Claude neatly. *How do you do?*

Elodie could feel the heavy presence of Luc-Pierre at her back. She stepped forward to sit beside Claude, but Nora grabbed her hands.

Do you see? she shrieked. *Do you see what you have made? But how did he . . . how can this be?*

Nora let out a wail and gestured to the workbench. It

held the nicks of a decade's toolmarks, and when Elodie looked closer she saw that each groove held dark red stains.

The mechanism is a simple one, said Nora. *I've never known someone to perform the process on their own flesh, but it . . . I mean, it must be possible. The evidence sits before us.*

I have been waiting, Mme. Selkirk, said Claude, standing up and taking Elodie's hand in his own. *I was waiting for you to come and collect me.*

Not knowing what to do, Elodie let her hand be taken. Through her glove, Claude's skin was as cool as morning dew, and she could not help but let out a sigh.

My own brother, croaked out Nora. *My own flesh and blood. And now he is . . .*

Now he is not, said Elodie. The words felt heavy with realisation. *He is something else.*

Now he is nothing at all, said Nora. Her eyes met Luc-Pierre's as he stood in the doorway.

Luc-Pierre creaked out several coughs before he could speak. His voice sounded fleshy and wet, as if he had half-chewed liver caught in his throat.

What shall I do, Mme. di Haviland? Where have I to go?

But Nora could not reply. Luc-Pierre held her gaze for ten beats of his heart, then turned and walked out on to the street.

Elodie neither saw nor heard any of this: all she knew was the calm, clean angles of Claude's face.

Is this what you wanted? she whispered to him, under her breath so that Nora would not hear. *Is this what you wanted all along?*

I want nothing at all, said Claude.

Over the following months, the happy couple were never out of one another's sights. Nora closed the shop for a week and the city's gossips revelled in the slump of her shoulders and the reddened skin around her eyes, but when she re-opened the shop they soon forgot. Business was as breathless as ever, and Nora had to take on two ladies to help with the shop floor while she worked on repairing the boys in the back room.

She did not call on her friend, but Elodie barely noticed, too busy staring into Claude's shiny eyes and selecting new items for his trousseau. She also did not notice Luc-Pierre lurking in the alley outside her apartment in the moonlit hours.

The neighbourhood cats circled around his ankles hopefully, willing him to break into song so that they could join in, but they were left unsatisfied. A few times Luc-Pierre tapped on the front door, but always hurried away before the maid answered it.

When Elodie heard that Luc-Pierre had been spotted jaunting around the town with Cara O'Donohue, her only thought was a gladness that she would never have to tell a fortune again. Every night she removed the stash of gold coins from Claude's belly, and every morning she fed them to him once again.

By mid-winter, both Elodie and Cara sported eye-wideningly large rings on their engagement fingers.

One January morning, barely two weeks after Christmas, the happy couples happened to pass one another on a street corner. Elodie and Claude strolled in perfect rhythm, their hat-brims parallel to the sky; Cara and Luc-Pierre trotted in a mass of frothing ribbons and ruffled shirtfronts. As they passed, the ladies tucked their gloved hands further into the crooks of their lovers' arms, bobbing their heads to one another in congratulations. Their smiles were as wide as crescent moons.

Good morning, Mme. O'Donohue, trilled Elodie.

And good morning to you, Mme. Selkirk, replied Cara.

The men blinked an acknowledgment of their prizes. They all saw Luc-Pierre's foot edge out into the space between the couples, but it was too late to stop Claude from toppling into the leaf-choked gutter. Luc-Pierre kept Cara's hand caught in the crook of his arm and walked away without blinking, his back pointing straight up to heaven.

GIRL #18

Girls #1-17 were no good at all. They'd been coming to the door in the weeks after the accident, but never for anything in particular. There was nothing left to bring, nothing to say. The bouquets had withered days ago and the cards still perched on the mantelpiece, the same as our birthday cards had for the last eighteen years. I wondered if we were supposed to send thank-you notes to acknowledge them. A part of me wanted to enjoy it. When else was I going to have every girl from school knocking on my door? But the absence of Ishbel weighed on me, weighed in me, like I'd swallowed a handful of pebbles, and that made it hard to feel anything at all.

But now I'm shoeless on the beach and it's spitting with rain and the wind is pushing screeches into my ears, and there's Girl #18. She's standing a few metres away along the shore. Right away I know she's different from Girls #1-17. I open my mouth to say hello, but the words won't come. I try for a polite cough, but it sounds like dropping gravel down the gutter. The girl looks up and I almost bite off my tongue.

All the other girls had had plenty to say. *Ishbel's room,* they'd said. *Just a wee look, to remember her. I made* – At this they tugged something out of their handbags, like a piece of card busy with scissor-curved pictures of the two of them, faces flat and open. I used to know the girls' names once – used to chase them around like a puppy after a stick. Now they were just a mass of shiny hair and shiny shoes and shiny handbags. *Come in*, I said, and moved out of the way.

I expect the same thing to happen with Girl #18. The forced words, the distance between us. But instead I can only stare at her. The scar splits from her right temple to the bridge of her nose, like her face is a badly-done sketch that the artist crossed out. The scar-crossed eye is sewn shut, but the other one peers at me flatly, blue as an enamelled dish.

With all the other girls, I had let them upstairs and gone back into the front room. Dad was watching the telly with his hands cupping his knees and Mum was polishing the little crystal animals again. I slid down on the couch so the leather farted and tried to hear what the girls were saying over the drone of the TV. They probably weren't saying anything at all, because what do you say to an empty room? I wondered whether I should ask if the girl wanted tea or something, because although no one really likes tea, we all make it for one another out of politeness, like shaking hands. I rubbed at my throat where it hurt. There was a fat line of scar and stitching and I avoided that, but there was also a shiny-soft bit, the size and shape of an acorn, where the stubble wouldn't grow any more. I stroked that soft patch with my thumb until I couldn't feel it.

After each of the other girls had left, I went into the kitchen and made four cups of tea, then threw one into the sink. Then I remembered that I hate bloody tea and threw another one in the sink too. Then I remembered that Dad would only let his go cold and Mum would try to polish hers like the crystal animals, so I chucked the whole sodding lot in the sink and sat in the back garden where the wind dragged the water from my eyes.

Girl #18 stands with her feet in the water and smiles at me, so wide that her scar crinkles and makes the tip of her nose flatten. Then she turns and walks forwards, into the sea.

She used to stand on the shore. Ishbel, I mean. She planted her feet on the sand with the waves sucking at the soles of her wellies and she told me about all the other shores she could see.

Reykjavik. Svalbard. Cape Farewell.

Once she said she could see Labrador and I said that sounded even more made-up than Cape Farewell but she insisted that it was real. She said it was in Canada and I still thought she was bullshitting me but I couldn't say for sure because Ishbel read maps like storybooks. She was getting off the island, and no one was going to stop her. That was all just romance, just fairytales, because anyone can leave the island. Since they built the bridge, leaving should be as easy as sticking your keys in the car ignition. But leaving is never easy.

Girl #18 is in the water up to her knees, and I'm struggling towards her through the freezing shallows, the sand tugging at my soles. With every exhale, like a mantra, I say *Ish. Ish. Ish.*

I passed my driving test on the day after my 17th birthday – *our* 17th, it should have been, but Ishbel always liked to be difficult and had hung around until after midnight to be born. She had never managed to pass her test, though she'd tried five or six times. She couldn't do all the things at once, like changing gear and pressing the pedals and looking in the rear-view mirror. She was too busy looking forward, trying to see over the next hill. She always lost her concentration and her foot slipped off the pedal, and the car grumbled to a crawl, and she could never understand why. So she made me drive her. She jangled the keys in front of me in a way that was supposed to be fun, to tempt me into adventure, but when I scrunched up my face her expression slipped.

Please, she said. *My eyes ache. My feet itch.*

And I still thought she was being melodramatic but I took her anyway because all my mates were chatting up girls round the bus shelter and I had a cold sore that I didn't want anyone to see. We'd already made an excuse to our parents and clicked on our seatbelts before I thought to ask where she wanted to go.

I don't care, Angus. Just keep going until we bump into something.

Like Labrador?

Like fucking Labrador.

I turned the key and headed away from the lights.

Girl #18 is in the water up to her chest now, but I've made it in deep as my waist. Her scarred side is turned away from me, and in the fading light I see that she is not beautiful. Maybe that's when we see the truth of things, when all the beauty is stripped away.

Tourists laughed at the BEWARE OF SHEEP road signs, like the sheep were in armed gangs or planting terrorist bombs or something, and we laughed at them too. So when I hairpinned the car round a corner and a curly-horned blob of wool was stood slap-bang in the middle of the road, my first instinct was to laugh. That can't have lasted more than a second because then Ishbel's hand was on the wheel and I felt it tug under my palms and my head thudded against the window and then the ground was the sky was the ground was the sky was nothing, nothing at all.

~

The sea is cold enough to push the breath from my lungs, but the girl's head is still above water. When I drag her out I'm shivering so hard I think I might choke. She follows me back home, her feet soft on the sand, her hand held tight in mine. The whole way my heart throbs in my ears but she is quiet, so quiet. In my bedroom she stands in the middle of the floor and peels off her dripping clothes, letting them fall to the carpet. When she's finished she doesn't look naked. Not sexy or vulnerable. She looks like she is meant to look. She raises her head, gazing into me with that one blue eye, so close I can almost see myself reflected.

I go into Ishbel's room. All the furniture was pushed to the edges when we had the viewing, because even big bedrooms don't usually have enough space for a coffin. No one has been in to put stuff back so I have to wriggle in behind the bed to get to the wardrobe. The first items I can reach are the most recently washed things. Ishbel's favourites. I let my knees bend until I'm sitting on the bed, and I hold the pile of folded cotton in my hands. It doesn't smell of Ishbel. It smells of laundry detergent and that faint mustiness of unaired clothes.

I edge out of Ishbel's room and go back into mine. The girl is standing as I left her, and I want to say that she looks exactly the same except that she doesn't. It's like I've been away for months, years even, and in that time she's grown and matured way past anything I could ever be. She's an adult. A woman. That's the thing about girls: they're never really girls at all. They're always women really.

I dress the woman in Ishbel's clothes, and we're only inches away so I can see her scar as close as I see my own face in the mirror. It's the same colours as Valentine's Day flowers: pink and white and red, swollen and rounded like petals. I lean in, my hands in my pockets, and press a kiss to the scar.

It is cold, because she is cold.

Outside, I put my keys in the ignition. The woman stands outside my car door, her hand held palm-up like she's waiting for me to hand her something.

Right, I say, *of course. Sorry.*

The words come out clear and strong, and as I swallow I can feel the gravel shifting in my throat. I climb out and go around to the passenger side. By the time I've climbed back in and fastened my seatbelt, the woman has started the engine. The car grumbles against the soles of my feet. From the passenger side the world seems to have tilted, like that game where you close one eye and then the other to watch the world leap.

Behind me is the silent house, polished crystal animals, cups of tea topped with tepid milk-scum. In front of me is the twisting grey road to the bridge. The car moves forward, and it's too late for me to stop it. Maybe it's always been too late.

A few metres from the start of the bridge, I start to cough. The woman pulls the car onto the hard shoulder, but doesn't stop. She takes her foot off the accelerator so the car rolls forwards at walking pace, wheels chewing the loose ground.

I open the door and lean out, the seatbelt hugging my shoulder. I cough and choke and feel something scratch up my throat and clatter onto the road. Without thinking I close my mouth to catch the last of it then tuck it behind my bottom teeth. It feels hard and sweet.

On the road behind me, the things I've coughed up look

like nothing, just a mass of grey that you'd kick over like pebbles. As I watch, it shrinks out of focus. I slam the door.

When I face forwards again, the car has crossed the bridge to the mainland. I am the only occupant.

I slide over the gear-stick to the driver's seat and press my fingers to the acorn-sized scar on my throat. The whole of Scotland is blanketed out in front of me – and who cares that I'll eventually just bump up against a different coast?

There are always other places.

There are always bridges.

I turn the key and head for fucking Labrador.

UNA AND COLL
ARE NOT FRIENDS

UNA

I'm not going to sit in here with Coll. They can't make me, they just can't, and they say it's because I'm distracting but that's not fair because Coll is distracting too, so why should I have to look at him? Shut away in this wee room together, like we've got foot-and-mouth or something. It smells like old porridge and permanent marker in here, and everyone else gets to sit in the big airy hall that's got windows and radiators that actually work. I don't want to be distracted either, and it's giving me the boak the way that Coll's tail-tip twitches like that when he's thinking. I know that nothing on me is twitching, so I can't possibly be as distracting as Coll.

Oh god, look at him now. Any normal person would be chewing on a pencil while thinking about that maths problem – and I knew it's Question Nine he's stuck on, because it's a total doozy – but not Coll. Oh no, he's sat up straight in his chair, totally motionless except that the tip of his skinny wee tiger-tail is quivering and jittering right at the corner of my eye. He's tucked it through the hole in the back of his chair and it's swaying in the air, curling up

towards his head but way behind his line of sight. He probably doesn't even know he's doing it. Not that that makes it
okay, obviously, because it still distracts me.

Miss! I shout out, *Miss, he's putting me off my test!* and
even though Miss McConnell patters right over she's not
listening to me, she's – what a cheek! – she's shushing me,
like I'm the one causing a ruckus.

But Miss, I say, *it's Coll, miss, his tail is –*

And then I stop talking because Miss McConnell's
jumped back as if I've slapped her. I'm not looking at Coll
but I can see in my peripheral that he's leaning back in his
chair with a big grin across his chops.

You can't, sputters out Miss McConnell, *it's not –*

And I know what she's mad about, it's because no one
ever mentions it directly –his freakishness, his malforma-
tion, his 'special difference' – but I'm sick of having to go
to another room for no reason when I'm meant to be doing
my stupid Maths exam.

So I look her in the eye and I say exactly what I know
she's thinking: *Coll's a weirdo, miss!*

And Miss McConnell's eyes aren't looking at me. They're
moving up my forehead, past the top of my head, up-up-up
and I know exactly what she sees. She looks at me and she
sees a weirdo, just like Coll. She's put us in here together
not just because we're distracting to everyone else, but
because she thinks we belong together. She thinks we
should be friends because to her we're the same. But we're
not the same. I pick up my pen and I throw my test paper
at Miss McConnell (even though I know half the answers
are total bumf) and I storm out of the room, and the whole
time I'm thinking: Coll Bailey, I will never be your friend.

COLL

Una Geddes was a right laugh today. Shouting at Miss McConnell then pure storming out of the test room. Nice for me to get a bit of peace to finish off the test, anyway. Question Nine was a right pain in the bum. I took the long way home today so I'd go past Una's house, just to get a look at what she was up to. I had to walk practically round the whole island – in January, and all, with the snow all crunchy-solid and the sky as grey as your granny's knitting – but I didn't see Una.

She used to be all right, Una, when we were kids. I liked that she wasn't fussed about her antlers. When you're wee it's okay because kids just get on with it, but you know what it's like when you get older. Any little difference gets pounced on and picked apart – and we had some pretty big differences, me and Una. For years I asked my Mum to sew special bits on my trews, like wee zip-up pockets in the bum area or a channel of fabric going up my back to tuck it in. It was no good though; I couldn't sit down properly, and everyone knew it was there anyway. After I while I thought – screw it, everyone knows I'm a freak anyway, so I might as well just carry on with things like it doesn't exist.

But Una, she wasn't like that. Well, there's not much you can do to hide bloody great antlers stretched a foot out of the top of your head, but still. She never bothered with that awkward phase. It was almost like she was proud. She'd wrap coloured scarves around them and hang necklaces off the curly ends. All the other girls fussed around her, painting patterns on them with their nail polish and that. She was so friendly, Una. She'd be pals with anyone. Except me, obviously.

Mum! I shout as I open the front door and dump my school bag on the couch. *I'll be in my room!*

I thump up the stairs and jump from the doorway onto my bed – I can do some epic leaps, cos my balance is better than most people's. While I pull off my school tie I soak up the applause, bowing to my imaginary audience.

I put my feet up on the radiator and wonder what Una's up to right now. I've got big plans for the night: beans on toast in front of Corrie, then a Halo marathon with my wee bro. Oh aye, rock and roll. I bet Una doesn't watch Corrie. Actually, I bet her Mum makes her wrap wire round her antlers and stand behind the telly to get a better reception! Nah, that's harsh. I wouldn't want her to know I thought things like that about her. But she called me a weirdo, and I'd never call her that.

Everyone thinks we should be friends, me and Una. Because we're alike. Because we're different. It's a shame she's such a cow.

UNA

I don't really know why I hang around the whisky sheds. They're unheated, and there's no one to talk to, and if I get caught my mum will go totally mental. The whisky sheds are these massive low buildings made of dark wood, with tiny wee windows. They're surrounded by barbed wire and there's never anyone around. The whisky casks get stacked up in there and left to mature for years and years. They're sort of creepy, actually, and maybe that's why I like them.

It's bloody freezing though, and it's literally impossible for me to wear a hat. My nan used to knit me special hats – they were more like a band of wool to go around my ears, really – but she died a few years ago, and I don't like to look at those hats any more. So instead, I just have to hunch up my shoulders in a tragic attempt to keep my ears warm. My toes went numb ages ago and it's difficult to get my boots into the gaps in the fence, but I manage it. It's stupid to come here. But you know the worst bit? I can't stop thinking about that stupid Coll Bailey.

He's such a pain, always distracting me when I'm just trying to get on with my work. I hate how people think we're going to be Best Friends Forever and get married and have weird little babies. Ugh.

But I suppose it was just a tiny bit sexy, the way he leaned back in his chair, and when I ran out I could feel his eyes on me, that big grin . . .

But oh my god, gross, never would I ever. This is COLL BAILEY we're talking about. I shiver, and not from the cold.

I creep silently down in between the row of sheds, and then I straighten and walk properly, scrunching my feet through the new snow, because there's no one here anyway. I'm just getting into that idea – that it's just me, totally private, alone with my noble thoughts – when I see movement in the very furthest-away shed.

S-l-o-w-l-y, the door wheezes open. Not like that fake squeaky sound that doors make on telly, more like a cough that's been held in for ages. I shouldn't be here. I should NOT be here. They're going to catch me and they're going to prosecute me and my mum is going to go totally, absolutely, literally mental.

But peeping out from inside the shed, bright against the snow, I see the tip of a tiger tail. And that's when I explode.

COLL

Coll bloody Bailey, what the bloody hell are you doing? Una

65

speaks in this sort of whisper-shriek, like she's really mad but doesn't want to make too much noise. I feel like the cold has frozen my jaw solid, but it can't have because I've only just got here and wasn't really outside in the snow long before sneaking into this shed. It was a bit warmer than outside, but with Una standing in the doorway the temperature seems to have dropped fifty degrees. I'm not sure whether I should lean on one of the casks with one elbow, like in a suave Don-Draper-from-Mad-Men sort of way, but I don't think it'll look right in my parka and bobble hat.

I traipse across half the island to find you, I say, *and this is the thanks I get?* Too late, I realise that is NOT what Don Draper would have said.

You bloody well did WHAT, Coll Bailey? whisper-shrieks Una, and she puts her hands on her hips like she's some-one's mother. She has to let go of the door to do that and it whacks her on the elbow, but she doesn't flinch. Then she marches towards me, arms akimbo, with a face so angry it could scare off a storm.

She gets right up in my face, all ready to scream at me or bite off my nose or something, and just to stop her I lean in and press my mouth against hers.

Her lips are the warmest, softest things I've ever felt.

She jumps, and I count one-two-three, waiting for her to pull away, but she doesn't. And then, weirdly, she's smiling. Her lips are still pressed to mine and so it makes me smile too.

I've always thought that Una moved more slowly, more gracefully than other girls – maybe because she's got to carry that extra weight on her neck – and now I see how that grace is in her kissing too.

After some time that feels like forever and also like a

millisecond, Una pulls away. Then she pecks her head back towards me and dots a kiss right in the centre of my lips.

Tomorrow, she whispers. *Here*. And then she's off, striding ankle-deep through the snow. I run to the doorway and catch the door before she slams it, so that I can watch her go. She glances back, and the beginnings of the sunset gleam colour into her cheeks.

Coll Bailey, she shouts back over her shoulder as she scales the fence, *I will never be your friend*.

THE GRACEKEEPER

The graces are restless today. They pweet and muss, shuddering their wings so that the feathers stick out at defensive angles. I feel that restlessness too. When the sea is fractious like this – when it chutters and schwaks against the moorings, when it won't talk but only mumbles – it's difficult to think.

I spend a little time, an hour or two perhaps, sitting by the house and watching the clouds. Many boats passed yesterday so the sky is cluttered. I watch a shiny red tug pass, coofing smokeballs up to join the other clouds.

There's a Resting due this afternoon and I must go inside to prepare. The grace is ready; when I enter the house he's huddled in the corner of his cage, head under his wing, feathers puffling around the wrought iron prayers of the bars. He knows that this is the closest he'll ever get to the sky again. *I know the feeling*, I tell him, and drop five sunflower seeds into the cage.

Before the Resting party arrive I take the raft out and feed a few of the graces. I'm not supposed to, of course, but some people deserve a longer remembrance. I've seen their families – the quickness in their smiles, their relief when it's a small grace. Real grief, and I don't feed the grace: I know those people don't need the grace's death to tell them when mourning is over.

I eat bread and honey, drink a bone cup of milk about to turn. Supplies will arrive with the Resting group. A large box of body, a small box of milk and socks and soap: this is all the world sends across to me.

I should go and visit mother, I know. But the last time I visited she barely knew me, and I fear that the next time she will not know me at all. It will not matter to her whether I come today or tomorrow. It will not matter to her whether I come at all. I must prepare for the Resting now, and there is so much to do.

The Resting was brief. I whispered the words and brought out the caged grace, moored it to the wooden box as the family watched from their craft. The children clutched their pockets and the widow gazed at the grace as if willing it to live forever. I will not feed this grace; they will not sail back to check if it still breathes. When the grace dies, they will be allowed to forget.

The widow thanked me afterwards with her damp swollen hands too tight on my wrists, speaking in fummels and haffs as if she could not get enough breath. Her wedding ring dug into her finger, making the flesh bulge out at either side, and I wondered whether she would wear it until it was engulfed: her own secret totem, shined black tefillin lashed tight to arm and thigh. I watched from my window as they sailed back to shore.

Sometimes when the boats sail away, I feel that one end of a fine thread is tied to the boat's bow and the other to my ribs. With every beat of the oars I feel something over my heart stretch, and stretch, until it might break. A string like the one between the wooden box and the grace. At those times I take care to turn away, to busy myself with moving supplies onto the shelf, to hum so loud my throat burns, to remind myself that I am here.

I will visit mother tomorrow.

Every night I lie awake from the pale blue of dusk to the pinkening of dawn, and my eyes will not close. Finally, in the darkest part of the night I get out of bed and lie with my feet in the water, feeling the waves lick up my calves. Somewhere between sleeping and waking, between floating and sinking, I slip into the water. I float among the graces, watching the toenail-clip of moon reflect off the cage bars. Lying back I let the sea hum into my ears, stroking at my hair, telling me stories in a series of takas and whooms.

I imagine my mother in her tower room, landlocked, swaddled in blankets. Her skin crinkled soft as paper folded, unfolded, refolded a thousand times. I wonder if she even knows me any more, or if I have become just another confusing memory. Perhaps the thought of me is a spiderweb: too thin to be gripped, just shreds clinging to her hair.

I imagine my mother imagining me, and just for a moment I feel the nudge of her fingers against my knuckles. Opening my hand, I feel her take it. We float there in the hush of night.

When I was a child I talked of chunks of land floating on a globe of sea, held by road-thick ropes fastened to anchors the size of castles. I asked my mother what would happen if the ropes were to wear away, if the countries were to bump and jostle one another – if one might attach to another, if bridges might be built where only sea had been before – or if the edge of one would tip under another, upending it like a toy tug carrying too many pebbles at one end. Your brain is upside-down, my mother said. Land does not float on sea; the earth is a solid mass like a rubber ball, and oceans sit in cups carved out of land. Land decides water, not the other way around.

Lying on my back among the graces, limbs spread wide as a starfish, I feel I will fall up into the clouds. I reach out for something to hold on to, but there is no other hand there: nothing solid in this gap between earth and sky.

Weeks have slipped by on my chunk of land and today is the Resting I have been sickening over for months, for always. I choose the biggest grace I can find and rub at its cage until it gleams like fresh pennies, but tears are salted and I must repolish three times before it is ready. I did not visit and now I cannot look at what is in the box, to see her eyes misted over and her jaw sunken back. Instead I say the words over and over in my head until they lose all meaning.

I wonder now why other Resting parties let me say the words. They let me recite them like poems learned at school, knowing that I do not apply them to the scrap of person in the wooden box or to the burning star of their loved one's memory.

So I look down at the box, and I say the words, and for the first time I understand them. My last link to the world has gone. I know what it means to be a stranger.

In the pinkening dawn, I swim out to mother's grace. I open the door of the cage and watch the grace spread its wings, watch it sputter out until it is nothing more than a comma among the clouds. I duck my head under the water and swim for shore.

SLEEPING BEAUTY

THREE

A few months later, queuing for cinema tickets with her new boyfriend, she sees him. He's walking down the street – headphones on, eyes down, click-clacking a Zippo. The sight makes bile rise hot in her throat. She pretends to examine the cinema posters and blinks until her eyes stop watering.

By then, she'd already decided not to tell. Silence is easier, that's all. She has no proof and wants no fuss. It's not even a crime, not really. Nothing would happen except that she would never be herself again. She'd be That Girl. Did you hear? She was asking for it.

Besides, she tells herself, she'll forget. Like she forgot how long to cook a soft-boiled egg, the nickname her dad used to call her, where she'd hidden her journal. Any day now, she'll forget.

TWO

She wakes with his fingers inside her.

She stays perfectly still, her breath sleep-slow. She's not scared. More curious. The room is still spinning and half-

72

dreamed thoughts argue behind her eyes. Her body feels heavy, numb. His breath is hot on the back of her neck.

She tries to breathe. Slower. After a minute he presses himself closer, pushes his fingers further.

Maybe he doesn't know she was asleep. Maybe he thinks that's why she invited him over.

But it isn't.

This isn't.

She's going to say something. She's going to sit up and punch him in the jaw and tell him to get his dirty fucking hands the fuck away from her. She's going to scream right in his face that she's not a piece of goddamn fucking meat. She's going to. She's going to do it right now, and before she even stops doing her fake sleep-breathing he rolls away from her and he slides off the bed and he goes into the kitchen. She hears the tap running, a glass filling, and he comes back into the room and he lies down on the floor and pulls his coat up over himself like a blanket. She stays awake until she hears his breathing slow.

ONE

What's your favourite fairytale? he says, passing her the joint. Another night, another stupid question. His random statements, his tired attempts at quirkiness; everything about his personality bores her.

Who's your favourite Beastie Boy?

Would you rather eat shit or vomit?

What's the best kids' TV show?

Sometimes she invites him over to watch DVDs or listen to music, but this time it was just because he has hash. If she can just get a bit high, then it'll be worth having to talk to him. The last time she invited him over, he stayed for a whole weekend, asking her stupid questions and drinking all the milk. She can't be bothered with that tonight. She'll try to get rid of him quickly, just as soon as this joint is finished. And maybe one more, for luck.

Well? he says, flicking the Zippo in that cute way he has. It makes her notice his hands, the shape of his thumbs; she's always found guitar-players' hands sexy. Maybe she'll kiss him later, if he stops being so annoying. She holds the hot smoke in her lungs then blows it into his eyes.

I don't know, she says.

WITCH

I met Baba Yaga at the end of childhood – past pigtails and fairytales, but not quite ready to give up on make-believe. We had always known that she was there. She was the centre of every scary story our parents told us. They said she had a thousand eyes and watched us as we slept; she had goat's feet and a rooster's beak and creepy-crawlies in her hair. She had a fence made of bones and a huge cast-iron oven for roasting nosey children. Every detail made us want to see her more. I dreamed of breaking through her hedge of thorns to find out what she kept at the top of her chicken-legged hut.

I dare you, said my friend Emmy one night, and that was all it took. No double dare needed. At sixteen, it was very important to be louche.

Sure, I said, my mind exploding with the secrets of the chicken legs and the goat's feet. I could already picture Baba Yaga's face, waxy lipstick smeared and hair a rose-bush tangle.

I knew Emmy only dared me to get a reaction. We'd fooled around a few weeks before, and now she was being all weird, playing mindfuck games. The way I saw it, she had started it all, plying me with her mum's stolen booze and sucking my tongue on the roundabout in the children's playground. Everything was spinning so fast, I'd had to kiss her back to keep from falling off the edge of the world. Her mouth tasted of schnapps and peach lip-gloss. She kissed like a bank robber, like she was trying to get in and out as fast as possible. Even with the grope up my top and through the zip of my jeans, she was done before the roundabout had slowed to a stop. I'd wandered home, streetlit and frustrated, then rubbed my clit while thinking of Emmy straddling me on the swings. The heat of her. The soft skin. The secret wet places. And then it wasn't Emmy but someone else, a woman not a girl, older and stronger, knowledge seeping out of her and into me like the sweet drip of honey, and I came so hard, gasping out a name, and ever since then it had been weird between Emmy and me.

The dare came two weeks later, a Tuesday night towards the end of the summer holidays. We were bored. It was August, still warm in the twilight of 9pm. We'd made the most of a bottle of Jack, sipping back and forth as we wandered the suburban streets. For a while we'd peeped in windows, but it was too early for anyone to be in bed, and that was the only room that interested us.

It didn't take long for us to bump up against the woods. They weren't even woods really, just a few acres of scrubby trees bordering the town.

That's where Baba Yaga lives, said Emmy, her voice thick and slow from the alcohol. In my mind, Baba Yaga was the bitch goddess warrior queen. She terrified and fascinated me.

I dare you, said Emmy, and I was lost.

When I come back, you're buying vodka.

If you come back. Emmy drained the bottle then pressed her lips against mine. The whisky burned, and I pulled away and walked into the woods without looking back. I pictured Emmy, so small among the trees with the empty bottle in her hand. She'd wait for me.

I planned to walk to the other side of the woods, then come around the edge and creep up on Emmy to give her a fright. She was pissing me off, but I still wanted to fuck her, and I figured making her squeal and jump into my arms was a good start.

It should only take about twenty minutes to walk around the edge of the trees. I grinned at the thought of Emmy, still waiting there. She'd already be regretting her dare. She was probably wishing we were back at hers, sprawled on her bedroom floor, smoking joints and sliding our tongues into each other's mouths. Even though we had to jump apart every time her mum thumped up the stairs, messing around with Emmy still did it for me. Once I'd given her a good scare, maybe I'd let her take me home.

It was darker here among the trees, and the sounds of the town were muted. I could smell wet earth and woodsmoke. At first my progress had been stilted, every other step kicking into a bit of litter or clump of twigs, but the further I got into the woods the clearer the way became. The humidity was getting to me, my T-shirt sticking to the small of my back. I wiped the sweat off my forehead with my palm, feeling the burrs and bits of dead leaf stuck in my hair. Without realising, I was walking more carefully, trying not to make the leaves crunch under my feet. The woods looked the same in every direction, and it seemed like darkness was falling faster. I started to wonder if I'd somehow turned myself around. Digging my feet down into the carpet of leaves, I closed my eyes and listened. Maybe if I could hear some noise from the town, I'd be able to figure out where I was. Soon I heard something that was not a night bird or a burrowing rodent or the distant murmur of traffic. It was the noise I had dreamed of Emmy making.

I opened my eyes and crept towards the noise as quietly as I could. The moans and rustles grew louder, and I ducked down when I saw the gleam of naked skin. I held my breath and watched. Through the screen of thin branches I couldn't tell what combination of male and female I was watching, but I knew the rhythm of that motion. The moaning turned into words, a vague mumbling, oh-god-oh-god-oh-yes-oh-fuck. I shifted my position, squatting so that my heel pressed up against my swelling clit. I rocked as I watched, thinking about how Emmy was going to make those noises later when I slid my fingers inside her. I imagined the sweat on the couple's skin, bellies sliding together as they thrust, the feeling of being filled, of slickness and hardness, and I pressed my heel harder against the knot of fabric in the crotch of my jeans, and I thought about sucking earlobes and kissing throats and biting lips. I felt a pressure building, the air catching in my throat, the throbbing growing to a peak, and as orgasm shuddered through me like a wave across a rock, my foot slid out across the leaves.

The couple stopped abruptly, jerking up like lions interrupted while feeding. Oh shit, I'd been spotted. I tried to make my exit with the speed of running and the silence of creeping, somehow managing neither. After a few minutes I dared to look back – I was alone. I let out the breath I had been holding, then inhaled the musty smell of the woods. For a while I leaned against a tree, feeling grounded by the bark scratching against my palm, until I was ready to move on. Sure, I had almost got busted for peeping, but that had only made me more eager to get back to Emmy and re-enact what I had just seen. I let a smile slide onto my face, and headed off in what I thought was the right direction.

In front of me stood a concrete hut, long abandoned, covered in 'Danger of Death' signs. The council must have forgotten it years ago – it had the unmistakable squalor of 1970s' architecture. I barely glanced at the greying bricks before continuing. I was eager to get back to Emmy for our night of scaring squealing kissing fucking. And that would have been that, except as I was walking past the door of the hut, it opened. Outlined in the doorway was a woman with a head of heart-red curls and arms full of chopped wood.

Oh, she said. She looked at me for a moment, then stepped back inside the hut and closed the door.

I stood stupidly, breathing the smells of rotting leaves and cool air, and stared at the closed door. Every time I blinked, I could see the after-image of the woman: her red hair, her purple dress, her dirty bare feet. My head throbbed with alcohol and heat. For all I knew, there was probably some awful reason why the woman was lurking about in the woods in the dark. She could have been burying bodies; maybe she had a bloody axe to go along with that wood. Maybe she was waiting in her hut for some stupid kid like me to come along and be worm-food.

None of this stopped me from knocking on the door. For a long time nothing happened, and I was suddenly aware of how ridiculous I looked, slack-jawed and half-drunk in my dirty jeans, knocking at the door of an abandoned hut in the middle of the woods. I looked like an artist's reconstruction of a scene from a true crime book. Then the door opened.

The woman was still holding the chopped wood in her arms. The lights behind her lit up her hair like a bloody halo.

Yes, she said, *you saw me. You weren't expecting it, and neither was I. So let's just get on with our lives and pretend that this never happened.* She frowned, and it was the most beautiful thing I'd ever seen. I couldn't let her close the door on me again.

You're her, I said. *Baba Yaga.*

The woman raised her eyebrows and looked down at herself. *Do I look like I have goat's feet and a rooster's beak? This hut may be ugly, but it's not on chicken legs. And I assure you that I don't spend my nights riding around on a giant broom.*

Those are just stories they tell kids. Probably so we don't come here and find you. Because you . . .

Because I what?

Because you're the bitch goddess warrior queen, I thought. *Because you want to be left alone,* I said.

And yet, here you are. Not leaving me alone.

I smiled with one side of my mouth, in a way that Emmy had told me was extremely fuckable. This seemed to be a universal feeling, because Baba Yaga smiled right back.

You might as well come in, she said.

Baba Yaga showed me around her home, the walls hung with saris and the cupboards full of books. She explained to me how she had soundproofed the walls and stolen a generator from a poorly-guarded building site. Most of all, she told me how she had come to be the wicked witch: an eviction from her flat, a girlfriend running off with her boss, a three-days-drunk stumble through the woods. An empty hut, a new life. She told me how she had sewn stories around herself: a shroud of children's nightmares to protect her from the world.

I told her stories too. Her stories were about building things, making a life; mine were about emptiness and drifting. Just sixteen and done with school, done with parents; living in a squat and drinking my way along the suburban streets until the lights started to blur. I had come unmoored, but now I'd bumped up against her.

When we'd finished talking, Baba Yaga kissed my throat and dragged me to bed. I had spent my childhood fantasising about her – the images left in my head after my bedtime stories. I had dreamed of fairytales, and she was better than all of it.

I pulled off her dress, the bright fabric catching in her curls. I fumbled, laughed, was silenced by her mouth on mine. In one movement, she shook off her clothing and tore off mine. Her skin was hot and smooth. She licked her way down my body, her tongue as rough as a cat's. I wouldn't close my eyes, desperate to see every moment of her. She slid her hands under my hips and lifted me. I wrapped my ankles around her head and pulled her into me, but Baba Yaga only gave what she wanted to give. She pulled away, teasing me. On her knees at the end of the bed, she stretched her body out for me. The pink of her nipples, the soft weight of her breasts, the angles of her chin and wrists and calves. I could smell her cunt, a scent like the ground after rain.

I crawled towards her on the bed, sliding my body under hers, pulling her down onto me. She was honey on my tongue. She was the poison apple, the kiss that would wake me. When she finally slid inside me, I knew the end of my story. I never wanted to leave my bitch goddess warrior queen. I knew what happily ever after was, and I wanted to be a wicked witch too.

By the time I got to the edge of the woods, Emmy had gone. I only went to tell her not to wait for me any more, so when I saw that the street was empty, I turned around and went right back home. Back to Baba Yaga. Over the years, I sometimes wondered what had happened to Emmy; how long she'd waited that night before turning away from the woods; whether she'd come in after me or just got bored, wandered off, and forgotten. I wondered if she remembered that night in the children's playground; those sticky, blurry kisses. I wondered whether she'd ever found her own witch to love.

Parents still tell their children bedtime stories: two wicked witches, perched in their chicken-legged house, hiding away from the world.

ALL THE BETTER
TO EAT YOU WITH

'Once upon a time,' the big one said, 'this was all ice.'

'All of it?' the little one said. 'Even the bits trapped up on shore with the crabs and beasties in? And the waves coming in and the white bits all the way out? And those faraway bits past the islands?'

'All the way out to sea it was,' the big one said. 'But there was no sea, you see, only ice. There were wolves too, and the wolves would prowl around on the ice and nose right into the door of your house, bold as you please! What do you say to that?'

'They wouldn't come in our house,' the little one said. 'Because in our house there's you.'

'Well,' the big one said, 'that may be so. But what if those hungry wolves managed to get a wee nip at you anyway, hmm? Because as you know, my tidbit, the wolves love nothing more than the crunchy-munchy bones of little ones – just – like – you!'

'I think that would be not so bad,' the little one said. 'Wolves' bellies are soft, I bet. And I have sharp nails. I could claw my way out.'

'Oh yes, my morsel?' the big one said. 'And if the wolf bit off your fingers?'

'I'd bite his right back. My teeth are even sharper.'

'And if he pulled out your teeth?'

'I'd kick and hit and headbutt him all to pieces.'

'And if he bit off your legs and your arms? What of your pretty head?'

'Oh, don't make me say it.'

'You must say it. You must say it so that I know you know.'

'I'd use you as a distraction so I could escape. You're my secret weapon.'

'That's right, my delicacy. And what must you care about?'

'Nothing. Only myself.'

'When the time comes, you'll remember that, won't you? For the seas are no longer ice, but the wolves are no less hungry.'

THE MAN FROM
THE CIRCUS

1

I stepped out for a cigarette halfway through the girl-on-the-pony show. I liked the idea of the girl-on-the-pony show, but the reality of it depressed me. I could see the gobs of glue holding on the horse's plume, and the girl had lipstick on her teeth.

It was all 'no smoking' here, even round the backs of the tents, so I had to go all the way to the main entrance. It was quiet there, the music and applause muffled through layers of canvas. The night smelled of popcorn and diesel fumes. A ticket collector lurked in the background, his booth lit with strings of Christmas lights. He probably hadn't seen anyone for hours; no one would arrive at the circus this late.

I was down to my last cigarette. I patted all my pockets before remembering I'd left my lighter in my other jacket. I went to pluck the cigarette off my lip when a lighter flickered, spotlight-bright in the darkness. I know, right? It's like something off the Classic Movies channel. I leaned forward and lit my cigarette, closing my eyes so the smoke wouldn't burn.

Thanks, I mumbled around the filter. The lighter snapped shut, and I could see who had offered it. His features were uneven: his nose a little too flat, his eyes a little too small. He was TV-ugly – imperfect, not the romantic lead, but still attractive.

I didn't say anything, just exhaled some smoke rings. I was playing it cool, my cigarette in one hand and the other tucked in my back pocket, my hips tilted towards him. His pick-up routine was lame; but hey, I was eighteen.

Would you like to go for a ride? he said.

I flicked away the stub of my cigarette: it hit the gate and rebounded with a flicker like a Bonfire Night sparkler. He took that as a yes, and walked away from the gates.

The man from the circus whistled a tune as he tapped his fingers along the row of cars by the kerb. Maybe he thought that if he distracted me, I wouldn't notice that he was breaking into the car rather than unlocking it. I knew that shiny red Subaru well; I watched Willy Murdo polish it in his driveway every Sunday.

I couldn't stop staring at the man's earlobes. I know it's a weird thing to say; they were just so big, stretched out like doughnuts with wooden things in the holes.

He opened the passenger door and stood beside it. Did he want me to drive? He looked impatient; if he'd had car keys, he'd be jangling them. I opened my mouth to make an excuse, then realised he was holding the door for me. Another Classic Movies act. It made me wish I was wearing a fancy hat and very shiny shoes.

He pushed the driver's seat back as far as it would go, but his knees still barely fit under the steering wheel. He didn't look that tall out under the sky, but he looked huge folded inside the Subaru. He fiddled around under the steering wheel, then spun the wheel and roared into the night.

The town was pitch black: no stars, no house lights. Everyone was inside the circus tents. The only lights were from the Subaru, directing us through the hills. I hoped none of the sheep had wandered into the road. I didn't want to die with only a sheep and a very tall man from the circus for company.

The silence stretched, longer and darker than the road ahead of us. I opened my mouth to tell him to watch out for sheep, but it sounded stupid even inside my head. I ran through other possibilities: what kind of music did he listen to, where was he from, what was the circus like? I could tell him about how bored I was at school, how much I secretly hated all my friends, the way my eyes itched every time I looked out at the mainland. I didn't want to say any of those things.

Last week, I said, *on the radio, there was a competition. The DJ played a sound-bite of a car going over a cattle grid, and people had to phone in to guess which cattle grid it was. I didn't phone in, but I knew the answer.*

I waited for the man to tell me that in the circus there were no radio competitions, no DJs, no cattle grids. He didn't say anything. I watched him and he watched the road.

Looking back, he must have said something. There's no way I would have done what I did with a man who had only said a few sentences. But I've played it over in my head, and the only words I remember hearing were my own.

I need smokes, I said.

The man from the circus nodded, and the road wasn't there anymore. I must have drifted off, because there was the petrol station, lit up like the *Titanic* in the middle of the night.

The man's long fingers touched everything in the garage. He couldn't just look with his eyes; he needed to touch things to get a sense of them. He touched the packets of crisps and magazines and bottles of windscreen cleaner. He flipped through the air fresheners – even though they were all the same – and placed one carefully on the counter.

Twenty Lambert and Butler, I said to the slack-eyed boy behind the counter. Maybe he was sour-faced because he had to miss the circus. I wanted to tell him that he hadn't missed much, but that wasn't really true.

The man from the circus pulled a note from his pocket and placed it carefully on the counter, then walked away. His long legs had carried him back to the car before the boy had even opened the cash register. I'd expected his money to be unusual somehow: folded into an origami swan, or scrawled with magic symbols. I scooped up the change, cigarettes and cardboard tree.

Back in the car, I held out my handful of coins. The man spread his hands.

I have nowhere to keep that.

I saw that his trousers were a smooth length of fabric – no pockets, no seams, not even the zip of a fly. Maybe they were special circus trousers, ones he could change by folding bits in and pulling cords. I stuffed the coins in my pocket and handed him the Magic Tree.

Do you always buy gifts for the people whose cars you steal? I said, peeling the cellophane off my cigarettes.

I never steal. He smiled with one corner of his mouth, like it was caught on a fish hook. *I borrow.*

He jiggled something under the steering wheel and the

car lit up. He tied the Magic Tree to the rear-view mirror and flicked it with his fingernail. We watched it spin, the yellow cardboard bleached white in the floodlights. The man grinned as wide as a skull.

Ready to go? he said.

I looked at the world lit up by the garage's lights: the black fields, the black sky, the black hills. The car idled, the engine ticking like a horse pawing the ground.

You must say, he said. *Say you want to go with me.*

I thought about the hush of the wind in the trees, the smell of the fishing boats, cattle grids on the radio. I thought about seeing more sheep than people. I thought about the eyes of the boy in the petrol station.

I want to go.

2

The harsh sweet smell of fresh sawdust, the hot salt of roasting peanuts, the bitter reek of the horse's box. The raucous symphony of the musicians tuning up, the one-two-three of technicians testing microphones. Faces half-painted: a paper-white forehead and glitter-drenched hair above pale lips and blotchy cheeks. The air thick with shreds of marabou feathers, the chatter of the strangers, spotlights reflecting glitter.

And me, watching the world lit by the border of bulbs around my mirror. This pre-performance is as familiar to me as Luka's face. It'll be an hour yet before I see him – like a superstitious bride, he hides away so I don't see him until we're up there, tense and sparkling above the flimsy nets.

I was not the first girl Luka stole away, but I was the last. After me, he said he didn't need to try again. He'd found what he was looking for. So now, every night for ten years,

I have thrown myself off a trapeze and trusted him to catch me. Every night, he has.

It's not that Luka didn't provide what he promised; after all, he hadn't promised anything. The circus has everything I'd dreamed of: sparkling under spotlights, flying across a stage on the applause of strangers, waking up in a different town every day. Of course, it's not always a new town: Britain just isn't that big. But none of the places I've visited have had cattle-grid competitions on the radio.

Painted and smiling, I balance on my trapeze. Luka is poised ten metres away, his muscles shining under the lights. The wooden circles in his earlobes twitch as his jaw clenches, unclenches, clenches.

The ringmaster, his moustache oiled to needle-sharp points, announces glory and wonder on the death-defying trapeze. I pull dusty air into my lungs and start to swing. As I build up my momentum, I smile down at the crowd stacked up in the tent. Blinded by the lights, all I see is a mass of teeth and eyes and restless limbs.

From the corner of my eye I see Luka, hanging from his knees, patting his hands together so the talc can absorb the sweat of his palms. I wait for the twitch of his thumbs that lets me know he's ready.

I curl my toes around the painted bar, spread my arms like wings, and let go.

For two seconds I'm weightless, helpless as a newborn with its cord cut.

Then Luka's hands are on my wrists, calloused and hot, swinging me round. Below me the crowd gasps, claps, cheers. I count the seconds until he lets me go, until I will soar back to my own bar, until I will clamber to my feet and bow for the crowd.

I count, but he does not let go. His hands tighten on my wrists. I climb his arms and pull myself up onto his bar. He climbs up beside me and we wrap our toes around the bar. The crowd is silent, breathless, waiting to see what we will do next.

Come with me, Luka says into my ear.

I look down at our toes, lined up along the bar, miles above the mess of nets and shed glitter and eyes of the crowd. *Where? There's nowhere to go.*

Let's go away from this island. To the other side of the world. An adventure, just us.

I clutch the rope with one hand and reach out with the other, my fingertips sliding round the shell of Luka's ear. He takes my hand in his and presses our palms together, like we're praying.

I look at the world below us: the restless crowd, the glare of lights, the motes of sawdust in the air.

Say you want to go, he says.

I think of babies and gardens and road trips. I think of staying up late to watch a midnight movie. I think not of running away, but running towards.

Then I let go.

FEEDING

Before moving to the Outback, I had no concept of darkness. I thought I did, sure: weekends spent in Shoalhaven were pitch-black and silent compared to the eternal neon of Sydney. But Shoalhaven had street lights, house security lights, the odd car on a midnight errand. Out here, we're the only lights for miles.

We're in bed by 10pm. We don't have jobs and can go to bed whenever we like, but it makes more sense to get up with the light.

I reach out for Shelly. The room is so dark that white spots dance in front of my eyes. All I can feel is a mass of fabric. She used to sleep in just my boxer shorts, her breasts soft and heavy against my chest. Now it's full pyjamas in all weather. I wiggle my hand between the layers of fabric, trying to find flesh. I haven't even located a button when she elbows me in the chest.

I wake suddenly, feeling like something has just gone down my throat. In a lifetime, the average person swallows eight spiders in their sleep. At that thought, I'm scrabbling for the lamp, blinking in the glare. Shelly's side of the bed is empty, the sheets crumpled back. Her pyjamas lie in a heap on the floor.

I try to shout, but my throat is sleep-dry. I cough, choke.

Shelly! My voice echoes in the empty room. Aside from a bed and lamp, we haven't furnished this room yet.

Shelly!

I hear a tapping outside the window. In the spotlight of the lamp, the room looks like a movie set. I take the stairs three at a time, the rough wood splintering my soles. I flip on the kitchen light. The back door is wide open, hanging motionless in the heavy night. I feel stupid, standing by the kitchen table in nothing but my underwear. I scrabble through a drawer, my hand searching for the biggest kitchen knife. I grip the handle in my sweaty fist, square my shoulders, and walk outside.

Shelly is crouched in the vegetable garden. Her skin glows white against the naked stumps of tomato plants.

Shelly. It comes out as a whisper. She doesn't react. I take a step closer, dropping the knife onto the doorstep.

Shelly. She turns. She's wearing her green gardening gloves, a trowel in one hand.

Peter. She smiles. *Could you pass me the compost bag?*

It's the middle of the night! What the hell are you doing? I thought you'd been . . . I thought something had happened.

She shrugs. I can't help noticing the way the movement makes her breasts bounce.

I just thought the tomatoes would be hungry. She stands, leans, grabs the bag of compost. She thrusts a glove into the bag and throws a dark handful over the tomato plants.

But why now? I ask.

The plants needed it. Shelly pulls off her gloves and straightens, her body spread out under the sky. She stretches her arms up above her head and I can see the hollows of her armpits, the ridges of her ribs, the skin tight across her hip bones. She walks over to me, her movements sliding like water from a gutter. She pushes me to the ground and straddles my hips. The ground is dry, the cracks in the mud large enough to fit a fingertip.

They need it, she says.

We make love in the glow from the open kitchen door. The sky is flat, a vast nothing above us. I dig my fingers into the cracked earth so I don't fall up into the empty sky. Shelly tries to pull me on top, but I stop her. I don't want her to touch the starving ground.

I spend the next fortnight in the second bedroom. If we'd moved here a year ago, this would have been Jeremy's room. Shelly and I call this room the study, the library, the guest bedroom: everything except the nursery. Even so, I've painted the walls butter-yellow so that they'll work for a boy or a girl.

Shelly spends every minute of daylight in the garden. Grass has not grown. Dandelions have not grown. She has planted carrots, cucumber, peas, lettuce, courgette: they have not grown. In our month here, it has rained once. I stay in the second bedroom, painting the walls with sunlight.

On this day I've been working since it was light enough to see, losing track of the hours in the rhythm of the paintbrush hairs splaying against the walls, the burn of turpentine in my nostrils. My stomach informs me that it's past lunchtime. I put my paintbrush down, wipe my hands on newspaper. I slide the window up, wedging it open with an old jam jar. I lean out of the window and my hand slips off the sill.

There's a small child in the garden. She wears her mother's sunhat and a white dress three sizes too big. I open my mouth to shout, and realise the little girl is Shelly. Barefoot among the naked trees, she looks like Thumbelina.

I go downstairs and into the kitchen. From the doorway Shelly looks human-sized. She feels my gaze and looks up. The sunhat casts shadows under her cheekbones.

Hungry? I ask.

She shakes her head, rams her trowel into the ground.

I crack ice from the freezer, pour milk into mugs. The heat outside is choking, thick at the back of my throat. I shield my eyes with one arm, trying to hold the mugs steady. Ice cubes clunk against the thick china. I stand next to Shelly, making sure my shadow covers her exposed skin. I hand her the only mug that still has the handle attached. She stands, looks up at me.

Thanks, she says. We grip our mugs and survey the graveyard of twigs.

What are you planting? I ask.

Whatever will grow.

I think: nothing will grow.

I say: *Something will. When it rains, all this will sprout up.*

I gulp my milk. The ice cubes leave a drop at the tip of my nose; Shelly laughs and dabs it with the hem of her voluminous dress. With a jolt I realise it's one of her maternity dresses. The white lace hem is dusted brown where she's been kneeling on it.

I love you. She stands on tiptoe and presses her mouth to mine.

I love you too, I say.

I finish my milk, kiss her freckled shoulder, and go upstairs to start sanding the window frame. With the window up I can hear the earth outside cracking in the heat.

Later, I go out to the garden. The only mug with a handle sits on the doorstep. The ice has melted, the milk turned yellow and curdled in the sun. I tip it into the sink.

I lie in bed, listening to the crunch of trowel against hard earth. The light faded hours ago, and the room's edges are barely visible. I ball up the bed sheets and kick them to the floor. I fumble to the window and lean out.

Shelly, I call into the black.

The crunch of a trowel, then –

Yes.

Are you coming to bed?

Yes. The steady crunch.

Can't you do that tomorrow? You've been in that garden all day.

The plants need it.

She digs; I wait.

Shelly. Please.

She stops. The clatter of a trowel thrown aside.

You're right, Peter. I'll come up to bed now.

I crawl back into bed and drag the sheets over my legs. In the pitch-black silence, sleep comes quickly. In my dreams, the crunch of a trowel.

I make dinner: boiled chicken, mashed potatoes, peas. If I make the food plain, maybe Shelly will manage to eat some.

She prods at her mashed potato, piling it up at the side of her plate until the tower falls and scatters her peas. She cuts her chicken into thumb-sized bits, then carefully shreds it with the tines of her fork. After twenty minutes, I get sick of looking at my empty plate.

Is the chook undercooked?

No.

So why aren't you eating it?

She shrugs. Her fingers look as hard and thin as the cutlery. I look at her until she meets my eyes. She picks up

96

a pea between forefinger and thumb, and places it on her tongue. She swallows.

Happy?

Her cheeks are so sunken that I can see the pea where she's tucked it. I wonder how long she can keep it there before spitting it out. She stands, catching her chair legs on the torn linoleum.

I'll wash-up. She puts her full plate on my empty one and takes them to the sink. I leave the room before she goes into the garden to spit out the pea.

The house is so quiet that I can hear myself breathing. I gave up on painting hours ago to stand, breathing paint fumes and looking at the window. I've repainted the room five times, but it's still not good enough. The sun is falling behind the back of the world, dying the ground. It looks like a battlefield, red and scattered with the bones of trees.

The crunch of Shelly's trowel had become so constant, like a ticking clock, that I don't immediately notice its absence. I lean out of the window, paint flakes digging into my palms, and scan the garden. Naked plants cower in the bloody soil, Shelly's trowel and gloves sit neatly on the doorstep. In the sun's last light, a pale glow among the roots.

I tiptoe downstairs, unaware I'm holding my breath. The dinner plates sit by the sink, bone-dry. I step over the gardening gloves and into the garden. I can feel the cracks in the soil with my soles. The tomato plants seem to bend towards me as I approach, their twigs rubbing together like insect legs. I blink hard, watching the inside of my lids: the sun's afterglow leaves fat orange tomatoes on the empty vines.

The light has gone. I rub my hands in the soil, feeling

for the pale glow. I feel the slick jelly of gristle and snatch my hands back.

Chicken bones.

I'm onto my last useable paintbrush and Shelly has snapped the handle off her trowel. We've run out of milk, bread and toilet paper. It's time for a trip into town.

This is a larger undertaking than it sounds, as the nearest town is 200 kilometres away. Our jeep has no air-con, and if driven for more than an hour solid, thick white steam leaks out from the bonnet.

Shelly hasn't worn shoes for a month, and complains when she has to squeeze her dusty toes into her sneakers. Shoes don't bother me, but the jeep does. It has been sitting in the sun all morning, and the red vinyl seats are almost bubbling. We sit on folded towels, but the heat still seeps through. I try to hold the steering wheel with my fingertips.

Once we build up some speed, the heat isn't so bad. The driver's window only opens halfway, but we still get a good breeze. Shelly presses the radio buttons. The music is full of static, but it is music. She taps her fingers on her knees, ochre with ingrained dirt. I haven't seen her wear those cut-off shorts since we were teenagers; I didn't know she still had them. Her bare legs look like daisy stems, the same width from ankle to thigh. She starts to sway in her seat. From the corner of my eye I see her mouth sneer up at one corner. Then –

It's a nice day for a – she cocks a finger at me – *white wedding.*

She pushes her ponytail so that the front of her hair raises up into a quiff.

It's a nice day to –

Start agaaaaain. We draw out the syllables, wailing in chorus. I turn to look at Shelly – her hair quiffed up, her lip in an Idol sneer. Laughing, I look back at the windscreen.

There is a rabbit in the road.

I slam on the brakes, the seatbelt pressing out my shout. Shelly's hands grip her knees, her knuckles tight. The car is still. A ticking noise comes from the bonnet.

Is it . . . ?

I shake my head: it was too close. I thunk open the door and walk around to the fender. The rabbit lies a few yards behind the car. Its head is perfect: brown and fluffy, with long ears and limpid eyes. The rest of its body is a flat red oval, leaking onto the tarmac.

Stay in the car, Shelly.

I hear her door open, then click shut. She stares at me through the windscreen, her face expressionless. She leans forward and switches off the radio.

From the boot I pull out bin bags and a shovel. I wrap the bundle in plastic and put it in the boot. I spend five minutes rubbing my hands on the towel from my seat.

We say nothing for the rest of the drive.

I pull up in front of the grocery store and switch off the engine.

I'll put it in the big bins behind the shop, I say.

No. Shelly's voice is too loud in the suffocating car. *I want to bury her.*

Shelly, we –

In the garden.

We buy bread, milk, toilet paper. We buy paintbrushes and a trowel. We buy a small metal box.

Back home, I bury the rabbit while Shelly is in the shower. I don't want her to see it.

We fall asleep as close as ears of wheat: chest to back, fingers entwined. I kiss the skin at the nape of her neck, soft like rabbit fur. I dream of nothing.

When I wake my hands are empty and I can hear the crunch of a trowel. I stumble across to the window. In the black night all I can see is Shelly's white back as she crouches over.

I feel my way downstairs and run my hand over the kitchen wall. I find the light switch, but my finger won't move. The crunch of metal against soil seems deafening. I close my eyes and switch on the light. I only open them when the crunch stops.

Peter. Shelly stands in the open doorway, the metal box in her hands. I know without looking that it is empty. I step back, scraping my heels against the wall.

Why? It comes out as a croak.

The plants needed it.

I lie in bed, listening to the metronome of Shelly's trowel.

I lift the pillow off my face. *Come to bed!* I shout.

Her voice floats up through the night. *Yeah.* It's barely a word, more of a grunt.

She's been in the garden since dawn. She doesn't even bother dressing any more, just kneels in the dirt until it coats her skin. Her palms are so rough that the calluses form ridges like the cracks in the earth. She doesn't wash, so our bed is full of the grit of ochre dirt, tiny dried-up leaves, flakes of skin from her sunburned back.

I clench my fists under the sheet. *Shelly! Now!*

She doesn't grunt, doesn't break her rhythm.

In the months we've been here, nothing has grown. Shelly has planted every seed we could afford, and they sit motionless under the topsoil, sleeping or dead. The nursery is finished, pristine and smelling of paint.

Last week Shelly threw away her maternity clothes. They swamp her, so heavy with fabric that she can hardly lift her arms. I haven't looked at her body in days. When I go into the garden, I keep my eyes fixed firmly on the top of her head. I can't even look at her eyes, can't bear to see the bones and shadows around them.

I think I shout for her again, but it might only be in my dream.

I wake to a tapping above my head, and think: that's not the trowel. The taps grow louder, banging on the tin roof like an out-of-tune orchestra. I look at the window, at the sky's odd motion, and realise. Rain.

I rub my dreams out of my eyes, cough up the words I tried to shout. Shelly's side of the bed is unwrinkled. Her pillow sits on the floor where I threw it. I know what I should do: look out of the window, then leap down the stairs three at a time while screaming her name. I stand up, neaten the sheets, step carefully on the edges of the stairs so I don't get splinters. I walk into the kitchen with my eyes on the torn linoleum. I go to the sink, turn on the tap, drink a glass of water. The rain deafens me against the windows. I take a deep breath and open the back door.

The world outside is green.

Grass carpets the earth, pea-pods shiver as raindrops hit, courgettes sit heavily like sleeping animals. The air smells like greenhouses and wet dirt. Everything is so clean. I walk through the garden, the grass spotting my feet with mud, leaves wiping my bare arms. The rain wets my hair and cools the night-sweat on my back. I raise my hands to feel the falling water, the rubbery leaves, the bright firm fruit.

Shelly lies among the tomato plants. Each tomato is as fat and red as an overfed belly. Her cheeks are concave, her collarbones so sharp they seem about to pierce her chest. Her belly is famine-swollen, tight and round in the cup of her hip bones. The rain falls into her eyes.

I pull a handful of grapes from the vine and jam them into my mouth, the juice running down my chin. I tip my head to the sky and let the fat raindrops wash everything away.

MOMMA GROWS
A DIAMOND

TEN

Momma was with the pony last night. Lily and me have him in the mornings, and we give him a wash with the shammy cloths and a soapy bucket so he's ready for Jade to look after him the next night. I think Momma must ride him too rough because he's always sweating and white-eyed when we get him, pulling tight at his rope and spreading his wide beige lips. He won't settle forever and ever, he just turns circles around the stake. Me and Lily get nervy watching him paw scoops out of the backyard soil.

Maybe a carrot, says Lily, *he'll calm for a carrot.*

She runs through the field and across the courtyard and into the house, and the whole way the sun leans bright on her shoulders and her dress blows out at the sides in a candystriped triangle. Even out here with my hands pressed to the pony's brush-rough mane I can hear Lily crashing around the pantry.

She won't find a carrot. I heard Opal say she was chopping them all up for a stew, but I let Lily go because I want it to be just me and the pony. I'd have Lily run clean across town and into Lake Pontchartrain if it meant I got more time with the pony.

He's stopped circling but his hooves still stamp, and I have to keep my feet back while I lean in so he doesn't squash them. The air smells of sun and dirt and pony hair. My throat itches with pollen.

The men pay to see the pony and Momma is there too, and Lily says she knows why. I do know but I don't know too. I don't think about it because it hurts my brain and Opal says that makes your hair go white. Like those old scientists, she says. I like that my hair is dark and shiny like a beetle's shell, and I don't want it white.

When Lily comes swooping back out across the yard she doesn't have a carrot but she does have three lumps of sugar, and I think the pony likes that more anyway.

It's dinnertime and Opal's chopping a stack of vegetables nearly as high as her hair, which is pretty high, *higher than angels,* Opal always says, but I don't think that can be true. Opal says a lot of things that aren't true. My last birthday I was about to blow out my ten candles and just when I took my breath Opal said, *there's a black moon tonight,* but when I ran to the window it was as white as ever, penny-shined, winking down at me. So I know not to listen to everything she says, but I still check the moon sometimes just to be sure.

Opal's singing that she's wild about someone called Harry, *the heavenly blisses of his kisses,* waving the chopping knife round like she's conducting a bunch of musicians, and it doesn't seem to match up at all with the sound of the piano from the front of the house but that's okay because I like Opal's version better. I hear Momma coming before I see her because she's singing the song too, wailing it along the hallway and jangling her bracelets in time. They're singing so loud that they even drown out the ring-dinging of the streetcars passing by outside.

Momma joins Opal at the counter, scooping up the chopped bits and dropping them into the pot. The kitchen is hot already, so hot that sweat itches along my top lip, but Momma stands right by the fire so she can stir.

Momma. I sidle up to her and tuck my hands into the waist of her skirt – she always tries to shake me off when I do that, says I don't need to be hanging on her all the time now I'm big. *Momma, you wanna play tonight? Dolls, maybe?*

I don't really like playing dolls any more, but I think Momma liked to dress them up and brush out their hair. She's too big for dolls, but then so am I, so maybe that doesn't matter.

I can't tonight, my precious one, she says, wiggling her hips so I have to take my hands away.

Please, Momma?

I tuck my hands back in.

My angel, you know I can't. I'm working. Now you go help Auntie Opal with them vegetables.

Can't I help you work, Momma? Later, I mean? Can't I?

She stops stirring and turns around and stands there with the spoon in her hand dripping pale brown water onto the hearth. She looks at me for a long time and I want to run away because she's never looked at me for so long without smiling. *No,* she says. *You can't help yet. Now go and play.*

Opal isn't singing now and neither is Momma, and they're not looking at me and they can't see the way I'm wobbling my lip, so I make a little sob noise to see if that makes them look at me but it doesn't.

I stamp my foot but that just makes it worse because

Momma sucks at her teeth and it makes a tutting sound, and I know what that means.

The pony will listen. He will understand. I don't dare slam the door behind me but I do drag my feet so Momma can see I'm mad.

Outside I jerk my legs from the knee so that my shoes fly off across the yard. The pony isn't there and I forgot that he's with Jade, and that makes me sad instead of mad so I just walk to the edge of the yard and tip my head back to stop the tears falling out.

Above me the sky is purple-black and as wide as the ocean must be, all the stars flicking like fish underwater. The courtyard is ridged like turtle's shells and I sit on the wall and rub the soles of my feet up and down, bending my toes against the ridges until the bones crack. I stay there until the night air has dried all my tears up, and then I run inside to help Momma make dinner.

ELEVEN

Everyone starts out as a flower. There's Lily, and Rosa, and Orchid, but that's hard to say so we just say Orchard but that's flowers too. Rosa is real little, only three or four and so shy she barely even talks. I'm 11 years and 2 months and 3 days so I'm the oldest and that means I'm in charge, which is a good thing too because Lily isn't so smart and if she wasn't born a whole week after me then she'd be in charge and everything would go to hell in a handbasket. Opal says that sometimes and I don't know what a hand-basket is, but I like the way it sounds.

When girls get older they turn into women, and women are jewels. There's Amber and Opal and Emerald, and then Momma is Ruby. That's the best of all the names, Ruby.

I've never seen a real ruby but Momma has a fake one set in a ring that one of the soldiers gave to her. That was before he was properly a soldier, before he'd gone away to the Great War and then come back with bits missing and his teeth always pressed tight together. I don't know what happened when he came back because Momma never mentioned him again, but she still kept the ruby in a carved wood box on her dressing table and she'd take it out sometimes just to look. She mostly did that when a noisy man just left and then she'd call me into her room too, which is a thing she almost never does when it's night-time, only sometimes when she needs to tell me about what a man is made of, which is okay for me to know now because I'm nearly a woman. Momma says I'll always be safe from men because I know them now. I didn't know them last year because I was only little but being 11 is different so it's good for me to see them. They can never break me or use me now. I know how to use them so I'll get there first and that's how it works. Someone will always be used but it won't be me.

But Momma says not yet, not yet, not until I'm older and I like that because I want to help out Momma. Maybe one day I'll get a ruby too. The war was the biggest ever and everyone says there'll never be another one like it so there won't be any soldiers coming back missing bits again. So I don't know how I'll get a ruby but I'll try.

Aren't you tired of being a flower, Violet? Momma says to me one morning from the depths of her bed. *Flowers crush so easy, baby, but nothing breaks a jewel.*

I like being a flower and I only came in here to get my books to do school with Lily, but I don't know how to tell Momma that I want to help but I want to be a flower too so I just nod yes.

Diamond, says Momma, *no one could ever break a diamond cos it's harder than bones.*

I just nod at Momma and go out of the room with my books digging lines into my hands, and she must forget because she doesn't call me Diamond again.

Me and Lily are doing school at the kitchen table. The cats are yowling and someone is shouting in the next street but it's pretty quiet. It's meant to be Math today but we hate Math and Opal isn't watching us so we do Art instead. Sometimes we're meant to look at pictures in books and then write what we think about them, but that's boring so we're copying the pictures with coloured pencils instead. That's almost like saying what we think about them.

Lily is drawing a picture of the face powder lady from a page in a magazine, using lots of pink for her cheeks. I'm copying from the same picture but I don't like the lady because her eyes look as flat as her hair. So I draw the bird from the face powder box. It's got a red head and blue wings and a long green tail that curls around like the bottom part of the letter y. Lily is using the red for the lady's lips now so I have to wait.

The kitchen table has got all these little grooves and dents in it, and I press my fingers against them in case they're secret messages from the other girls who have done school here. If I lean forward I think maybe I'll be able to see the pony through the window, but the sun is too bright and I can't see anything because it bounces off the glass in white dots that make me squint my eyes. I rest my chin on my hands and my fingers smell of pencils.

I look over at Lily's paper and she's printing words under the picture of the lady: J-A-Y-D she's printing and

I know what she means so I say, *That's not how you spell it, Lily, it's J-A-D-E like blade.*

Before I even finish talking Lily tumbles off her chair and throws the red pencil at me and drops her picture on the floor and runs out of the room and *You can't say!* she shouts back from the hallway, *it's my name and it's mine and not yours and so you can't say!*

And then I feel bad for Lily because the most she will ever be is jade and that's not valuable at all, it doesn't even sparkle, not like a diamond which is the hardest and prettiest of them all, and I know then that's why Momma chose it for me. It makes me want to stand up tall.

I pick up Lily's picture and smooth out the creases. She's still in the hallway and I know that because I can hear her crying, but when I go round the corner I see her sitting on the bottom step and her face isn't wet at all. When she sees me she lets out a big sob like she's trying to suck up a sneeze. I hold out the picture to her. *She's real pretty and you will be too,* I say, *and you can spell Jade however you want.*

Lily does a smile like she really doesn't want to, but then it spreads wider so her teeth show, and she jumps off the bottom step and grabs my hand and we go back into the kitchen together.

TWELVE

Momma said the coins are for milk and beignets, *just milk and beignets,* she said, *and in double bags too,* and I meant to get them, I truly did, but the comics were so pretty, every colour on every page, and so it made me not feel hungry any more just to look at them. I thought if I had one that was mine to take home I'd never be hungry again because I could look at it any time I wanted. Even if Momma was with the pony or Opal or one of the soldiers I could be full up on colours.

The man in the store has one eye covered with a black circle with a string that goes around his head. Lily says there's nothing behind that circle, just a sewed-up hole with no eye in it. She says it's from the war, but I don't think that can be true because he's never been by to see Momma. Momma says I can call her Ruby now I'm 12 and a woman but it sounds wrong so I stick with Momma. I think that maybe Lily is just trying to scare me, and I don't like that because the man in the store is nice. Sometimes he sneaks a hard candy into the bag and doesn't charge me for it.

On the counter in the store there is a glass jar of pickled eggs and I try not to think about how they look like eyeballs. Sometimes I wonder if the man keeps the jar there to remind him what he's lost. But people do buy the eggs, so maybe not.

Lily and I are over by the rack with all the comics, because by then I've already decided that they're more important to buy than milk and beignets. But there's a problem: we have to decide which one. It has to be the perfect one, one that will make the spanked tushes we will get not hurt any more, because although we accept the consequences that doesn't mean that we will like them. I like that word, consequence. It's something that Opal says but I'm not sure that she knows what it means. I've never seen her open the dictionary and she never helps me and Lily with doing school.

Lily points at one comic that has a bright blue cover and shows a little girl in a red dress sitting on a man's knee, and I don't like that at all but then I see that the man's hand is resting on the head of a shaggy brown dog with its tongue hanging out pink and fat as ham, so I guess the guy must be okay after all. I go to pick the comic up but a shadow falls over it so I stop. The man who owns the store has come out from behind the counter and he's squatted down between me and Lily with his one eye swivelling from one to the other.

Poor lambs he says *poor lost lambs so far from glory.*

We're just picking out a comic, I say because I don't like him being so close, he smells of lavender hair-oil and sweat and it makes the hairs in my nose burn, *we weren't going to take them, I swear.*

Lily's not saying anything at all, just standing with her fists full of comics and staring up at the one with the little girl on the man's knee, and it makes me mad that I have to do everything just because I'm the oldest.

I'll take you to glory, he says, *oh my lambs, my little lambs,* and then he opens his arms wide like he's going to scoop us up and Lily throws the comics at his face and grabs my hand and we run run run out of the store and into the street, past the shouting soldiers with their empty sleeves and past the writer-men grumping over glasses of gin and the air that smells of rotting bananas and the sounds of a dozen pianos clashing around us and we're spinning around balcony poles and we're almost home before we even stop to breathe, and Lily's half-laughing and half-crying and I am too because I know we just got away from something but I don't know what.

We flatten out some newspapers from the gutter and sit on the kerb outside the house. I hear the church bells ringing in the distance, and I wonder if they're more than just a way to tell the time. I don't know what else they might mean but if it's to do with the man and his empty eye then I don't want it, I don't want it at all.

Momma says that me and Lily can't have supper because that's what the milk and beignets were for. I came home with the money still in my pocket but, *you can't eat coins,* says Momma, *so you march right back to that store.* She has her hands on her hips and she's looking right in my eyes and not sway-dancing or jangling her bracelets or anything, so I know she means it.

I won't go because of the man with the empty eye, but I don't want to tell her that in case of scolding. I cry and cry but she still just stands there so after a hundred thousand years of crying I tell her about the man and how he scared me and the bit about the poor lost lambs and then Momma wraps me up in her arms and lets me tuck my hands in the waist of her skirt like I used to, except I'm tall now so it's not a good angle but I don't care because it's Momma, it's my Momma and she makes it all okay.

Opal goes out and gets us all Eskimo Pies for supper, and me and Lily eat them on the back step with the ice-cream dripping from our fingers and it's the greatest thing I ever ate.

THIRTEEN

I'm at the table doing school with Lily when my blood comes. We're trying to read some old book about a man called Mr. Jackal and sometimes he's Mr. Hide and it's boring but at least it's not real long, and I feel something at the inside top bit of my leg, and I think I know it because Momma told me but I go and check anyways, and I want to go and get Momma but she's still sleeping so I don't, I just clean up and go back to the table and sit down next to Lily and open my book.

What's the matter? she says but I just smile all calm like ladies in portraits. I raise up my chin and think of the neat-painted lines of my face and I say, *Nothing, Lily. Let's read the story.*

Lily frowns and throws down her book and stomps out the back door, and I sit up straighter and turn the page, and that's when I know the difference between a girl and a woman.

I tell Momma about my blood later, when the sun has gone to bed and she has got up – they balance like that, like weights on a scale – and she comes downstairs to make me and Lily pancakes. The piano is already thrashing and rolling in the front part of the house and Momma swipes her feet across the floor in time as she's mixing up the batter. Her face is all painted and she keeps pressing her lips together to spread the red properly.

I wait until Lily goes to set the table and I sidle up to Momma and eat a fingerscoop of the batter, and I press my tongue to the roof of my mouth to feel the grit of sugar dissolving. And then, *Momma,* I say, *I'm a woman now.*

Momma stands, just stirring the batter, and more than anything I want to tuck my hands into the waist of her skirt. But that feeling passes blink-fast and right away Momma wraps her arms around me and strokes the strands of hair back from my forehead and, *A celebration,* she says, *to celebrate my little woman, all grown at thirteen.*

Momma lights candles and pushes them into the stack of pancakes and says I can lick the syrup straight from the jar, but I don't because suchlike things are for girls and not women, and Lily looks kinda confused but Momma tells her I am a woman and I just smile like the painting and I hope Lily's momma told her about the blood because she'll get a fright when it comes. I didn't get a fright and Momma fixed it all anyways and I'm so giddy with how much I love my home and my Momma and being Violet the flower-girl, and I push out all the thoughts that are making my forehead crease and I shovel pancakes into my mouth until they're all gone.

The week after my blood, Momma takes me into the front of the house and lets me meet the soldiers. One man has a body as round and soft as an uncooked bread roll. Another one is all elbow and knees, and his trousers are too short so I can see the knobbles of his anklebones rubbing on the rim of his shoes. Another one wears a long coat full of pockets and he limps on one leg – Momma says this is because he keeps his money in his shoe, but if he's got all those pockets why doesn't he put his coins in them?

Momma says soldiers used to be the best customers, that they were so proud she felt proud to be with them. She says they're still the best customers but now it's because they have to be. No one else will have them because they're broken, wild-eyed, likely to snap. Opal still takes them. She says it's a public service, doing her bit for the war effort. My momma laughs and says the war is over, but Opal says it'll never be over. It'll never be over when those men still have those eyes.

I think about if I'll raise my chin high like Momma or get on my knees like Opal, because I'm a woman and that's a decision that every woman has to make.

Momma puts red on my mouth and curls in my hair and tall shoes on my feet, and she holds my hand light as a moth as we prance through the house. The music is so loud it shakes my lungs and the floorboards sway under our shoes and Momma leads me on on on down a long corridor and through to a room with a huge rusted keyhole and she pulls a key from a hidden ribbon around her waist and she opens the door.

And I see.

I see what Momma and Jade and Pearl do with the pony. I reach out my hand and I stroke the pony, moving my hand in big sweeps like brackets surrounding us. From the other rooms I hear the crackle of a skipping record, some old song sung by a woman with a voice thicker than treacle. Outside, across the rooftops, I hear the church bells tolling from other people's lives.

The men around the edge of the room all clutch fistfuls of paper and I know, I know. I am a diamond and someday the pony will be mine.

THE LIGHT EATER

It began with the Christmas tree lights. They were candy-bright, mouth-size. She wanted to feel the lightness of them on her tongue, the spark on her tastebuds. Without him life was so dark, and all the holiday debris only made it worse. She promised herself she wouldn't bite down.

The bulb was sweet and sharp, and it slid down her throat with a feeling of relief: an itch finally scratched. She came to with a shock. At the realisation of what she'd done, she tangled the lights back into their box and pushed them onto the highest shelf. The next day she pulled down the box and ate the rest. The power cable was slippery as liquorice.

She got hungrier as the days passed. A lightbulb blew; she went to change it but ended up sucking it like a gob-stopper. She had soon consumed the rest of the bulbs in the house. Lamps mushroomed up from every flat surface – and there's no good in a darkened light. Each day she visited the hardware shop and walked home with bags full to clinking. Her eyes were always full of light; with each blink she caught gold on her eyelashes.

One night she opened her mouth to yawn, and saw that her path was lit. Up she jumped, pyjama-ed and barefoot, and followed the light across streets and playgrounds, fields and forests, all the way to the edge of the land.

She paused on the rocks, between the trees at her back and the black of the sea. This is where he left, and this is where she could find him again. She stretched her body to the sky in readiness, then opened her mouth to outshine the stars.

She spat out the bulbs – one, two; nineteen, twenty – in a runway from trees to shore. She spread herself out on the sand. A perfect starfish, a fallen body. An X, so he could find his way back.

MATRYOSHKA

Elimae was a magician with a key in her mouth, a foreign language, a matryoshka doll: uncomplicated on the surface, but with a dozen secret selves hidden inside.

She thought I didn't notice her, but she's all I did notice. All day I'd ring for iced water, sugared pastries, pots of blossom tea. Then I'd ring in the middle of the night just to see her stumble to the foot of my bed, hair twisted in rags and nightgown sleep-rumpled. I'd whisper my request so she would have to lean closer; so I could almost feel the heat from her skin. She'd bring me the extra blanket or glass of warm milk, then disappear back to her room, so tired she'd forget even to curtsey. I liked to think that my face, being the last thing she saw, smudged into her dreams.

I did not know what I was to her – a tyrant, a grasping child? – but I knew what I wished to be. Elimae was a matryoshka doll, and I did not want her surface: that painted design everyone could see. I wanted to pull apart each doll until I got to the one at the centre – the tiniest doll, the only one that couldn't be split in half.

When my brother Laurent turned 21, our parents decided it was time he found a princess – or rather, that one was found for him. At 17, I still had a few years of grace before I too had to be married off. To find Laurent's princess, our parents invited every lady in the land to a masked ball. Invitations were sent, the gold leaf indented into every letter by hand and delivered by a servant on a white horse. Responses were not necessary; no lady would miss a chance to become the next Queen.

I gathered my maids a month before the ball to plan my dress, my hair, my shoes. I asked them all what they thought, but the only opinion I cared about was Elimae's. Whatever she found beautiful was what I wanted to be. She was excused her usual tasks to work on my slippers, stitching pearls to the soft upper until it was too dark to thread her needle. While the castle slept, I crept out of bed and pulled out the shoes, lining them up on my knees. I kissed each smooth, warm pearl, imagining I kissed her fingertips. All I could think about was the night of the ball: Elimae dressing me, arranging each ribbon and ringlet, then standing back and seeing how beautiful I looked, my delicate feet in the slippers she made. I planned to send her to bed after that, carrying my image straight to her pillow. I'd have one of the other girls undress me after the ball, so that Elimae wouldn't see how my powder had smudged or smell the stale wine on my breath. Just for that night, I wanted to be beautiful for her.

Three days before the ball, and I was almost ready for display. The hairdresser had prepared a creation for my head: a cage of spun sugar around which my hair would be twisted and pinned, and which would disintegrate through the evening, scattering ringlets and glittering sugar shards onto my bare shoulders. The dressmaker had sewn three dozen jewels onto the bodice of my gown in the stylised curls of a peacock's tail. But the shoes remained half-stitched.

I rang the bell for Elimae with every turn of the clock's hands and asked about the shoes. The shadows under her eyes fascinated me, cinder-grey darkening to foxglove-purple. The night before the ball the shadows were the colour of charred wood, but my shoes were almost finished. I paused before dismissing her, watching the way she swayed in fatigue, wishing more than anything that she would collapse. Then I could take care of her: tuck her into the empty side of the bed, lay my hand on her sweat-itching brow, press my lips against her needle-swollen fingertips. But I could not touch Elimae, so I had to content myself with the last thing she had touched. I slept with the shoes cradled to my chest, dreaming of her fingers on the pearls.

The next day I could not sit still, not even for a moment. I wandered the wings and walkways, looking for Elimae. When I caught sight of her, tousle-haired and tired-eyed as a street urchin, I quickly looked the other way. She bustled past me and I turned to watch, desperate for a glimpse of the pale skin of her throat.

Three hours before the ball, my dressing-up game began. My serving-ladies made me into a mannequin, an invalid, a work of art. They passed in a blur, powdering and tight-lacing, but Elimae was nowhere to be seen.

Finally I was almost complete, perfect from my head to my ankles. I was standing on a wooden block to allow the dressmakers to re-stitch the hem of my gown, so I had a clear view of each tired head bent over its work. I was sure that Elimae was not in the room, and I couldn't bear the thought that she would miss my moment of beauty. As much as I wanted to stand there all night just so that Elimae could see me, I knew I could not. My mother, my father, Laurent; no one would understand that Elimae was all I cared for. I closed my eyes to hide my tears and stepped off the block – straight into my pearl-stitched shoes.

Without opening my eyes I knew that those were Elimae's palms pressing against my heel, Elimae's fingers easing my toes into the shoes. And, just as surely, I knew that these were not the shoes Elimae had been working on for the past month.

I'm sorry, she was saying, *my mistress, I could not finish. I'm sorry, I did try.* Her hands were hot and dry against my ankles as she slipped my feet into the soft blue slippers I wore every day to shuffle along the polished floors of the palace.

The gown is long, I thought; it will hide the shoes. I can make an excuse, I thought; tell my mother that I did not like the gleam on the pearls. I did not say these things.

Elimae, I said as I stood there in my worn blue shoes. And she would not look at me.

I waited, alone in my room, until the vibrations from the ballroom started to shake my spun-sugar cage loose. The sounds of the orchestra and a thousand dancing feet got steadily louder as I walked along the corridors.

Instead of parading down the wide arc of the main stair like the other ladies, I slipped through a side door, joining in the twirl of skirts as if I'd always been there. I made sure to take small steps to hide the scuffed heels of my shoes. I quickly found a man's hand to hold – as long as I kept a pretty smile on my face, he wouldn't notice my distraction. I did not even know whether I knew him; as this was a masque, his face was covered in that of a wolf. I rested my head on his shoulder and breathed in his smell of hair oil, starched cloth, and flower pollen. I felt it cloying on the back of my throat, but as long as I focused on him – the deep comb-ridges in his hair, his palm sweating onto my waist – then I wouldn't think of Elimae.

As was my habit, I was still searching every face to find hers. Silly, I know: she would be crying herself to sleep, or still desperately trying to finish stitching my slippers. I didn't want her to cry over me, but at least she was thinking of me. Perhaps I would visit her later. After the musicians had broken all their strings, after the dancers had hobbled home on tattered feet, after the whole palace was as quiet as a secret lover, I would tiptoe along the halls to Elimae's door. I would not knock, of course. I would creak open the door to reveal the tableau of a wretched girl: a tear-soaked pillow, patched skirts spread out across the bed, her tiny feet poking out of the bottom. Thinking of Elimae, all ready for me to save, made me smile and pull my dancing partner closer. His sweaty hand gripped mine harder, his fingers on the bird-thin part of my wrist, making the bones grind. I pulled back, keeping my gaze carefully away from his.

In the ballroom all the skirts billowed, all the bosoms swelled, but none caught my eye. The ladies' faces were disguised as swans, deer, pampered housecats. The men had all chosen to be wolves or dogs. I kept my eyes down on the floor, watching the dull glitter of shoes twisting round one another.

A flash of gleaming pearl.

I started, pulled away from my dancing wolf, but was dragged along by the force of bodies moving in sync. Had I imagined those shoes, those pearls I had kissed every night? I looked wildly around the room, trying to catch a glimpse of the shoes I knew so well. I had to know who had stolen my precious shoes, but all I could see were masks, blank and leering.

I let go of the wolf and forced my way through the shifting sea of the crowd, all toes and elbows. Pressed up against the wall, I stared around the ballroom. Nothing but twirling skirts and straining backs, then – there! The gleam of pearl. I kept my eyes on the swift movement of the shoes, upwards to a froth of white skirts, a tight-laced bodice, a single pearl nestled in the swell of breasts, and a mask of pale dove feathers. As the dancer turned I examined the line of her jaw and the angle of her wrist, trying to put them together into the shape of someone I knew. Someone who would steal my most precious possession. No, I amended, my second most precious – Elimae was surely the favourite thing I owned.

I kept staring at the masked dove, twirling gleefully in my stolen shoes. Belatedly I realised the identity of her dancing partner – my brother, Laurent. Dancing with the marriageable prince was surely making her the envy of the entire room. Laurent stretched out his arm to spin his mysterious partner, his smile obvious even under his lion mask. The dove turned under his arm, and as she pressed her body back against his, she looked straight at me as though she had been aware of my gaze all along.

I knew those eyes. Elimae, my matryoshka.

Everything moveable in me rushed to my throat, and it felt like a storm was thudding inside my head. I pressed my hands against the wall to keep from falling down. In the polished floor of the ballroom, the pearl shoes reflected to infinity. Had Elimae finished them and not been able to find me, and so had worn them herself only to show me how hard she had worked? Had she constructed two pairs, working double hours in secret, so that we might match?

Was she dancing with my brother because he was close to me, was my same blood and flesh? I could not think. I kept my back pressed up against the wall, the dancing figures blurring in front of me. The only shape I could make out was Elimae, shining clear as the north star in my brother's arms.

I stood in the corridor outside the ballroom for a long time. I stared at the polished floor, looking at my own tear-streaked reflection and trying to make sense of what I had seen.

It was not possible that Elimae could not love me the way that I loved her. What else could make her answer my ringing bell, tuck me into bed, arrange every lock of my hair? What else could keep her here in this castle? What else, but love?

The next day Laurent announced that he had found his princess. Elimae was displayed for the kingdom, paraded before the dukes and courtiers and footmen and swine-herds. I watched from my window as she trotted through the courtyard. Her dress was so long it covered her feet, and a jewelled tiara pressed her curls flat against her fore-head.

I stayed in bed all that day, and all the next. Servant girls brought silver platters of boiled eggs and tiny cuts of meat from songbirds. The textures sickened me; I pushed them onto the floor. The servant girls bustled around my bed, peering at me when they thought I wouldn't notice. I turned away from their faces: they all looked the same, all blank, all wrong. On the insides of my eyelids, Elimae's pearl shoes reflected a thousand times.

I heard the story carried in servants' whispers through

my door: a midnight tryst, a lost slipper, a chase across the county for the treasure of Elimae's hand. Spittle-flecked horses and her heel sliding perfectly in. I rang my little china bell through the night, keeping my eyes closed when I heard the door open so that I could imagine her tired eyes, her sleep-rumbled nightgown. But the smell from her wrists was all wrong. The voice, the sound of feet on the floor: all lies. I pulled the covers over my head.

Two months later, they were married. As Laurent's sister, I carried a bouquet and dabbed at my eye at the appropriate moment. Elimae wore an ivory dress and jewels in her hair. She glowed.

After the ceremony I escaped to the hallway, the floor just as shiny as it had been during the ball. I am convinced that my tear fell in the exact same spot as it had that night.

Elimae was a matryoshka doll, and I had not wanted her surface. I'd wanted the tiniest doll, the one at the centre, the one that could not be split in half. There she stood in her snow-white dress: unbreakable.

ORIGAMI

Another paper cut. Rebecca's hands were a mess: swollen with tiny cuts, peppered with dry patches. She'd have to make sure they were all healed before Sean got home, or he would know what she'd been doing.

She checked the clock. Almost six: she'd better get some dinner on. She pottered around the flat, checking the front door was locked and deciding which soup to heat.

Sean was supposed to phone tonight. It had been nearly a week, but the phones on the oil rig were always in high demand. Rebecca understood, even though it was a shame that they had such little phone time. At least Sean only did trips of a month: some of the engineers were away for six months at a time. Men with wives, children, pets, and friends they didn't see for half a year. No wonder there was a mad rush at phone time. The men must be so lonely, stuck in the middle of the sea with no one to love. Weeks of meals for one, falling asleep in front of the TV, watching happy couples in bars and shops and restaurants. Stuck in the middle of the city with no one to –

She was halfway across the living room carpet. She must have been wandering towards the TV, or maybe the bathroom. The cupboard was that way too, but she wasn't about to make that mistake again.

She hurried over to the cooker and took the soup off the

flame, the inside of the pan crusted with blackened chunks. The smell of burning filled her throat.

At five to eight Rebecca was on the couch trying not to stare at the phone. The pan, bowl and spoon were washed and drying by the sink; the TV tuned to a reality show. She was fiddling with the pages of the TV guide, but only because she was nervous about Sean's phone call. The pages were forming into fingers. With her thumbnail, she scored lines of knuckles on the paper fingers. She placed them carefully on the coffee table, then started folding some toes. The paper was thin and brightly-coloured, the knuckles creased across faces and times.

She resisted the urge to pick up the phone on the first ring. She carefully arranged the paper digits, then answered on the fourth ring.

Hello? She tried to sound husky, like she was halfway through a cigarette.

Hey, Becks.

Sean, baby. She bit her lip: that was too much. *How are you? How's work going?*

In the silence, she heard her muffled words back through the receiver.

It's good. Busy. Look, Becks, I've only got a couple of minutes. He paused, but she didn't say anything. The delay meant that they'd only end up talking over one another. *I'm really sorry, but they want me to stay on for another week. I wouldn't, you know, but we could use the money.* Rebecca listened to the clicking quiet after his words. *Becks? You there?*

Yes! Yes, I'm here. Sorry, the delay. I thought you weren't finished.

So it's okay? About the extra week?

Rebecca swallowed the lump in her throat as she stared

at the cupboard door. *Of course. You're right, the money would be nice. But you know* – she coughed. *I'll miss you. It's lonely here without–*

Becks, you won't – They both started talking at the same time, and had to spend a few seconds saying: no, you go.

Becks, it's just that – *I know it's stupid, but last time* – *I mean, that* – *you wouldn't, right? It's stupid to ask, but I worry about it . . .*

Rebecca's cheeks were blazing. Even though Sean couldn't see her, she did her best innocent smile.

Of course not. Don't worry, love.

I know. I'm sorry, I shouldn't have asked. Anyway, that's my time up so I'd better go. I'll call the day after tomorrow, same time. And Becks? I miss you.

Rebecca hung up the phone. She collected the paper fingers and toes and walked to the cupboard door. She closed her eyes, held her breath, and opened the door.

Later, halfway to sleep, she was pleased that she'd managed to throw the fingers inside without looking. Looking would lead to touching, which would lead to bringing him out of the cupboard, which would mean he'd be in the bed now. But it was just her, so she'd won. She wasn't lonely, she was victorious.

Rebecca woke from origami dreams, familiar shapes folding into strange forms. Eyes still sleep-glued, she ran her hands through her hair, feeling something hard and rough against her forehead.

Clenched in her palm was a crumpled paper hand.

Her whole body jerked. She threw the paper hand across the room, watched it sail through the air. It seemed to wave at her as it went, then lay silently unfolding on the carpet. She lifted the duvet, scanning the warm darkness for foreign body-parts. There was nothing but her own pale legs.

When her heart had slowed to a normal pace, Rebecca got up. She dressed without looking at the hand.

By the end of the day, Rebecca was exhausted. Avoiding paper might be feasible for a builder, or a sculptor, or a bartender; for a legal secretary it was impossible.

Much of her work was done on computer, so she'd thought she could manage; but she'd forgotten about the memos, post-its and phone messages that snowed onto her desk throughout the day. By mid-morning, her waste-paper bin was full of crumpled body parts.

But working hours weren't the only problem. During her lunch break, she paused mid-sandwich to fold intestines from her newspaper. Walking out of the office, her nervous fingers made an ear out of the tissue in her pocket – luckily the thin sheets wouldn't hold the shape, and unfurled as she threw it on the pavement. On the journey home, her bus ticket became a tongue.

When the bus reached her stop, she tore up the tongue and stuffed it down the seat. She kept her fists clenched as she walked home.

Rebecca was watching the news with her hands held between the sofa cushions. She'd tried to clear all the paper out of the house, but there was just so much of it: newspapers, novels, receipts, wrappers, bills, magazines. Different colours, weights, textures, patterns. Magazine pages were eyeballs: colourful, and held a shape well. Broadsheets were limbs: large enough for a whole leg. The TV guide had already become a pair of kidneys, and it wasn't safe to let her hands roam anymore.

Rebecca jumped when the phone rang, but she sat still until the fourth ring.

Hello?

Becky, hi. How are you?

Yeah, you know. Keeping busy.

Good. I'm sorry I couldn't call earlier. I queued for the phones every night, but I had to give up or I'd have missed my sleep.

That's okay. You'll be home soon, and then we can talk any time we want.

Rebecca listened to her muffled echo in the receiver, then the crackling quiet. She opened her mouth to speak.

Becks, about that. They offered me another week. You know you were unhappy with me missing New Year, and with the new shift pattern I'll be home right into the start of January. So it's better really, right? Becks? Rebecca?

Rebecca stepped back from the cupboard door. She was already at the full reach of the phone cord; to open the cupboard, she'd have to put down the phone.

I'm here, Sean. And it's fine. I'm glad you'll be here for New Year.

God, Becks, I'm so glad. You're not feeling...

Lonely, thought Rebecca. Lonely lonely lonely.

No, not at all. I'm actually going out with Jen tonight, so don't worry.

That's good. I put your photo beside my bed so I see you last thing at night and first thing in the morning. Your photo isn't very chatty though. I miss saying good morning and hearing you say it back. But look, I have to go, the phone queues are huge tonight and everyone's giving me the evil eye.

Okay. I love you.

Love you too.

Rebecca waited for the dial tone, then placed the phone

at her feet. She smoothed down her skirt, neatened her hair, and opened the cupboard door.

The man inside had paper hands, paper legs, paper lungs. He had eyeballs, toe nails, a paper heart. He was missing some bits – spleen, eyebrows, a left heel – but that didn't matter.

Rebecca helped him out of the cupboard, arranging him carefully on the couch. She flipped to the channel she knew he liked, and settled down beneath his arm. She nuzzled his cheek and stroked his broad, creased chest.

He was incomplete, imperfect. But he was here.

TIGER PALACE

THE TRAVELLER

Once upon a time there was a beautiful but cruel empress who lived in a palace at the centre of an impenetrable forest. The palace was carved from ivory with a tall central turret – so tall that the sun heated its metal tip hot enough to scald skin. Each window was made of jewels so the light shone a different colour into every room. And that's not even mentioning the empress, for she had skin that gleamed like polished wood and a mouth as wet and pink as the inside of a watermelon.

But the forest! We must not forget about the problem of the forest. Oh it was dark, and it was thick, and it was all set about with tigers. And not ordinary tigers, either: these ones had eyes that could see through the deepest gloom and claws that could scrape the marrow from your bones. Even if you got through the forest, the palace was surrounded by a wide moat full of alligators that trick you into thinking their lurking heads are stepping-stones. Stand on one, and – snap snap! – there will be nothing left of you.

At least, that's the version you've probably heard. That's what the traveller had heard too – but as she discovers as she begins her quest, the forest isn't impenetrable, just awkward. The vegetation is dense and stinking, and the scenery boring enough to deter most. Although rain never makes it down past the leafy canopy, everything is constantly damp and feathered with mould. But the traveller has sturdy boots and a ten-inch machete, so she makes it through the forest within a month. It helps that she can scent water even inside the spines of plants, and has no qualms about eating every part of the birds she catches.

Finally she reaches the clearing. Her eyes are open wide in the expectation of tigers, but she sees none. Perhaps they are hiding, she thinks – but tigers, as a rule, do not need to hide. As the trees overhead thin and disappear, the sun burns into focus. Between her and the palace is the moat, all full of alligators. But the traveller's skin is caked with sweat, and the shade of the palace looks as deep and cool as the bottom of the sea.

She pauses at the edge of the trees to sheathe her machete and suck water from her flask, which tastes stale. It might seem risky for the traveller to put away her machete, but there is a dagger in her ankle brace that she can whip out in under a second. She'll scent a tiger's fur or the sweat of an assassin long before then.

Now to face the moat. The traveller peers at the first stepping-stone for a long time, but she is sure that it really is a stone. She steps out, ready for snapping jaws.

Nothing.

She steps onto the next stone, and the next. She laughs aloud: not alligators after all, but stones to help her across. She traverses the moat in seconds, then kneels on the bank to splash water on her face, sucking the liquid where it soaks into her sleeves. Finally she stands to survey her prize. It seems so easily won, but now is not the time to worry about that.

The palace is wider than a hundred people could wrap their arms around, and it stretches so high that the tip of its turret is lost in a white-hot gleam. Each window shines a different colour, like a necklace of gems, and the traveller is sure – yes, there! – the empress is inside. She raises her fist and knocks at the open door.

THE EMPRESS

The empress's feet slide soft across the broken tiles, her slippers kaleidoscoping in shards of colour from the smashed windows. Years ago she'd played games with the light, making patterns and sending messages, but she soon realised that no one would ever understand them. She knows that many adventurers make it into the forest – she understands the birds, and oh how they gossip! – but few make it to the palace. Occasionally, every decade or so, she'll hear chirps about a pith helmet or the gleam of a machete, and she'll stand in the entrance hall in a pose of elegance. But when adventurers emerge panting and smug into the clearing, they're always a disappointment. So out steps the empress, and in rush the tigers, and then it is over. Until the next.

It has been so long since another living thing saw the empress's face that she cannot be sure whether she still has a face at all. Perhaps she is made of ghosts and glass now, the same as the palace. She fears that if she falls, she will scatter into smoke.

She drags her hand along the dirty wall as she walks. She feels the pressure of the stones on her fingertips, so she must be solid. She feels the itch of heat in her lungs, so she must be breathing.

A sound snaps the empress from her reverie. She listens

until the sound comes again, and again. Three knocks to herald her new visitor.

She hurries towards the entrance hall. By the time she gets there her breath is coming in gasps. The hall is big as a temple, its ceiling stretching up to dizziness. The floors are tiled grubby white like the rest of the palace, but the walls tell stories. Once the empress knew each one of those stories, but now they are just strangers doing strange things.

Through the wide entrance she sees a clear view of outside. She knows that the traveller sees china-blue sky and the burning eye of the sun, because once she saw that too. But that was long ago, before she lived in the palace.

She is not sure how the traveller will see her, but she knows that it won't be as she is: torn robes, tired eyes, a face saddened by the years. She positions herself by the entrance, peering out into the dim clearing, the light pale and dim as if her eyes are made of pearls.

There, the traveller! He is tired but not staggering, triumphant but not proud. The empress prepares to call the tigers – but she stops. Something is different about this one. Something is wrong. As the traveller tugs down his dust-veil, the empress sees the difference. Not a he at all, but a she.

The empress feels joy leap up her throat. A man cannot take her place, but a woman . . . Perhaps this will be the empress's last day in the palace.

THE TRAVELLER

The hall is a heaven of calm and cold after the choking heat of the forest. The floors are bright white, reflecting up onto walls that are a riot of colour and shape. The traveller blinks the dust from her eyes, and for a moment thinks that the beautiful woman before her is a mirage.

Madame, says the traveller with a bow, because it's better to bow for a mirage than ignore an empress. She blinks again and sees that the empress has an odd expression on her face, as if she is unsure of what to do next. The traveller hopes that she has not transgressed the usual social niceties – her time in the forest may have loosened her manners. Just in case, she bows again, deeper and lower so that her forehead almost touches her knee. The scent from the empress's throat is making her dizzy, so it helps to be closer to the ground. When she straightens, the empress has regained her coolly welcoming expression.

You may as well eat, says the empress.

This was something the traveller recognised. If you've heard the stories then this will all be familiar; if not, then let me elaborate. We have time while the traveller and the empress move towards the dining hall, for the palace is large.

The story goes that once the lucky and determined traveller makes it to the palace, a huge banquet is laid out. Each bite is the most wonderful thing anyone has ever tasted. The traveller feasts, the traveller sleeps. But the traveller must never, ever let go of his blade, as tigers enter the palace at the empress's command. In the blackest part of night, when the sun is at its furthest-away point, the traveller must leap up and fight the tigers. The battle is long and bloody, but the traveller wins. (The traveller must win, you see, or the story is over.) The traveller takes the empress for his wife, winning ownership of the palace and control of the tigers. And everyone lives happily ever after.

Now, you and I both know that this is only a story, and in reality the empress always calls the tigers to feast on the hapless adventurer. But this visitor is not like the others, and so perhaps the story that only the empress knows will come true. If all goes to her plan, she will have her freedom.

Ah – the empress and the traveller have made it to the dining hall, and we must rejoin them. If you were walking these halls you may have found yourself marvelling at the arched ceilings, or the gilt along each window-ledge, or the wondrous icy sheen of the tiled floor. You may have even found yourself swooning at the rich scents of cardamom and coconut milk from the dining room – or was that from the empress's perfumed throat?

But not the traveller. She is reminding herself about her blade, and how important it is to keep it close, and so she barely notices the glory of the palace or of her companion. She can scent her destiny on the air. Every step she has ever taken has led her here. To the palace. To the empress.

You may as well eat, says the empress, *and then you may as well sleep.*

For tomorrow, you see, she plans to walk out of the palace and leave the traveller in her place. But the traveller knows nothing of this. She lifts her golden spoon and prepares to feast.

INTERIM

The traveller keeps her hand on her dagger all night, but the tigers do not come. They do not come the following night, or the one after that.

Each night the traveller and the empress lay awake, fighting their own battles – one for a palace, the other for freedom – but each morning the dawn creeps in. They spend their days together, wandering the length of the entrance hall and discussing the meanings behind the stories painted on the walls. Every evening, after the sun slips into the forest, they surround themselves with flickering lamps and dip their hands into bowls of delicacies, their fingertips sugared and salted, their tongues numb with flavour. And then when they cannot speak for yawning they retire to their rooms, sure that tomorrow will be the day that it all ends.

And so the days became weeks, and the weeks became months – and still the tigers do not come, and still the empress does not leave. The empress and the traveller enjoy this life, and if they could choose they would wish it to continue. But they do not have that choice. Stories always have an ending.

The Empress

In the first few weeks of the traveller's company, the empress tries to catch her reflection in the oil-pearled surface of her bathing water, terrified that her glamour is fading. But she can never see herself clearly. The only way she can know how she looks is to check the response on the traveller's face – but the width of that smile never changes. So perhaps the empress has not changed either. If her false glamour is all anyone can see, who can say that is not her true face? The traveller is beautiful too, with her earth-brown eyes and muscles hard as cashew nuts. She will be a most comely phantom, the empress tells herself, and the tigers will be glad to have a new queen.

One night, sitting cross-legged on cushions with the lamps painting the traveller's skin in licks of honey, the empress hears a sound like a heavy curtain pulled back, and knows it is the sound of fate. She has been a beast for so long, and she is tired of trickery and glamour. She wants only this: to rest, to breathe, to live as if it were a choice. The traveller fills the silence.

The tigers, the traveller says. *They have not come.*

The empress puts down her cup and places her hand on the peak of the traveller's knee.

No, the empress says.

If I cannot fight the tigers, then I cannot win. The story cannot end.

The empress sighs and gets to her feet, standing tall so that her face is in shadow. She feels a chill around her shoulders and arms, as if the lamplight is a circle of warmth and everything outside it is frozen.

And so I cannot lose? asks the empress.

You may be wondering why the traveller did not try to end the story. Why she did not call for the tigers herself, whip out her machete and paint the walls with blood. But I have not been entirely honest with you about the traveller's reasons for her journey.

You see, the traveller knows the old story, the one she had seen in her picture books and heard at the fireside. She has been in love with the palace since she was a child, but now she loves the empress too. Most importantly of all, she knows that stories are what you make of them.

I know the story, the traveller says. *You must trick me, because I am a woman like you, and that means I can be tricked. Then I take your place in the palace and you are free to leave.*

The empress does not know what role the traveller is now playing, so she keeps quiet, her face in the shadows.

But what if I agree to stay? asks the traveller.

Then you would become –

A beast?

They both glance up in expectation of the tigers' distant roar, but no sound comes. The tigers are not there. Perhaps they were never there.

I will stay, says the traveller, *if you do.*

Impossible! says the empress. *Don't you see? There can never be two beauties. There must always be a beast.*

But the traveller's mind is made up. She had decided before she even set foot in the forest that this would be her ending. She knows that there are more reasons to go than stars in the sky, and only one reason to stay – but the empress gleams so brightly, and who can see the stars when the sun is out?

She takes the empress's hands in her own, leaning forward so that their mouths touch. They stay like that for a long time, until she has swallowed all of the empress's objections, all her arguments and trickeries. There remains nothing but the closeness of strange and familiar skin. As dawn begins to slip its soft fingers through the windows, the traveller pulls away and takes the empress into her arms.

And so, she says, *we will both be beasts.*

THE COMPANIONS

To the empress the night passed faster than a blink. Yet her muscles ache from being held so still and she can feel the gift of the traveller's lips against her own. She wants this to be their story – the press of mouth on mouth, the touch of skin – but she has never heard of such a thing. A story does not exist if no one has ever told it. Stories have authority; they cannot just be created from nothing.

You still wish to stay? she asks.

The traveller nods.

Go outside and look again, continues the empress. *Then tell me you would stay.*

They link hands and walk the length of the palace. The traveller pauses in the great hall, savouring the last time she will see the beauty of the storytelling tiles or feel the coolness of the air.

I will look, she says. *But I know that I will stay.*

She steps outside, into the deep cool of the shadows, and looks back at the palace. It still stretches to the sky, up up up as far as she can see. The windows still gleam green-blue-pink-orange.

She steps back inside. The air feels fresh and smells of summer rain. The ceiling gleams sun-white and the story-telling tiles are as bright as ever. The only thing that has changed is the expression on the empress's face.

She stands in the centre of the hall, gazing at the palace in wonder. She knows that she sees the palace as the traveller does, and that this is its true form. All around the entrance hall, each tile tells her a story of someone who had lived in the palace before. She sees each one clearly; each with its own beginning, middle, and end. They all left for the same reason that she wishes to stay.

I remember, she whispers.

Outside the palace, the forest sinks to the ground, smoothing out into soft emerald fields. The moat uncurls into a sparkling river, busy with fish. And there, ready to travel down the river to anywhere in the world, is a boat just big enough for two.

Once upon a time there was an empress, trapped as a ghost in the ruins of a jewelled palace, cursed to find another soul to take her place. At least, that's what the empress heard. But, as it turned out, stories can have any ending you like.

AUTHOR'S NOTE

Thanks to Mama and Papa Logan for always believing in me, and to Ross for the motivation of sibling rivalry.

Thanks to Annie Bennett for being my inspiration.

Thanks to Helen Sedgwick and Katy McAulay for workshops, wine, and not laughing at my terrible early drafts.

Thanks to Susie McConnell for four years of love and support.

Thanks to Aly Barr, Gavin Wallace and Emma Turnbull for always introducing me as a writer first and intern second.

Thanks to Cathryn Summerhayes for the badass agent powers.

Thanks to Chris, Jen and Tabitha from Salt for making this book so beautiful.

Thanks to Caitrin Armstrong at the Scottish Book Trust, Adele Patrick and Sue John at the Glasgow Women's Library, Joe Melia at the Bristol Prize, Judy Moir, Roxane Gay, Zoë Strachan, Louise Welsh, and everyone else who has helped and supported me over the years. Big kisses.